TREASURE OF ISOLDE

FREYA BLUE BOOK ONE

C.E. VINCENT

ISBN-13: 979-8-9883205-1-7 (Paperback edition)

ISBN-13: 979-8-9883205-0-0 (Ebook edition)

Written by C.E. Vincent

Edited by Stephen Parolini

For more information, please visit:

www.cevincentauthor.com

For my bold and fearless Luca. Thank you, gorgeous boy, for being the light of my life, and for inspiring me to write the stories I love.

1

The Hague, Netherlands

Walking across the Hague stage reminded Freya Blue of running into a stinging nettle bush in her beloved Congo; uncomfortable at first, but once she resigned herself to the pain, entirely manageable. Applause echoed throughout the proscenium, but it seemed like background noise compared to the clacking of her heels across the stage. Her sister, Jules, had dressed her in a god-awful blue wool shift by a well-known Italian designer who championed her cause. What was the name? Giada? Giancarlo?

She longed for the comfort of her trusty stained cargo pants as beads of sweat dripped from her bra line down to her stomach. Spotlights hit her eyes and it felt like she was staring into the sun. Speeches were easy for Freya. She rarely felt stressed when the work had to get done and important developments in her field had to be shared. But this audience was different; comprised not only of colleagues, but world leaders and noted environmentalists. What she said today would be shared on international news outlets, for the whole world to see. It could make her career. But she was using the podium for a different cause.

The many faces of the Hague audience came into focus. Government delegates, notable environmentalists, and the world's press had gathered for the three-day Environmental World Forum. Freya pulled at the clinging wool shift as an image appeared behind her: gorillas of the DRC she'd been researching and living with her entire life. As the thousand eyes stared back and the room quieted, Freya felt as though she was channeling her inner, rebellious teen, as though she was giving a big middle finger to the establishment that built her career. She grabbed the sides of the podium to steady herself. Maybe the pre-speech martini was a bad idea after all.

"Hello. My name is Freya Blue and I'm here to talk about my work in the DRC, my home."

The audience clapped again. While many attendees were at the event to further a cause they were passionate about, others attended out of some silent obligation or promises to constituents. It wasn't lost on her that her extensive study and documentation of primates and ancient cultures was only well known in her field's inner circles. As an Oxford student, her nuanced discoveries linking maternal behaviors between chimpanzee mothers and human mothers and subsequent publications put her name on the primatology map.

An isolated life in the jungle wasn't headline news. Still, she was accomplished enough to get funding and do the work she loved. The renown at such a young age had the odd effect of constant guilt. Her father, Howard Blue, had conducted similar research throughout his life and remained in the background. It didn't help that her sister, Jules, frequently reminded her that the fame was because she had privilege: pretty, dumb, blond privilege.

Freya gripped her notecards and turned to gaze at the image behind her. Her mind went blank, and she pushed the notecards aside. This event was her only chance to speak about something more important; something that would likely fracture her career, while creating the kind of dramatic change every environmentalist needed.

She'd waffled all morning about whether or not to take the chance. The expected speech was there in her notecards, in case she lost her nerve and couldn't do it. Being here was riskier than dangling from any cliff in the Congo because human beings hid how they killed each other off, whether by slow public humiliation or plain exile. At least in the Congo she knew death wasn't personal.

Her eyes searched the proscenium as the prolonged silence turned awkward. Audience members shifted in their seats. The lights from mobile phones documented her extended pause and apparent deer-in-headlights stare. But Freya's mind was back in the jungle. All she could think of was Nova. The proud lioness had caught a sixteen-year-old Freya unaware. In an instant, Freya knew what it felt like to know you were going to die, and then to be given another chance at life; to not be ripped apart by a pride protecting their young; to be chosen, instead, to protect them. *This is about them.* The move she was about to pull was career suicide. But in this foreign space with all these strangers, she couldn't help herself.

She looked to the sidelines where Jules stood and waved, a slight smile of encouragement crossing her lips. *Fucking say something, you stupid cunt*, she knew Jules was thinking.

Impatience ran in the family. Freya's eyes tracked to Jules' trusty assistant, the young and eager Gemma. Freya nodded to Gemma and the new grad furiously typed into her computer. The light shifted behind Freya as the image of the DRC apes was switched out for another.

Jules had worked her public relations connections to get Freya booked as one of the event headliners. She was always up for an impossible challenge. Jules thrived in pulling the delicate threads of high-profile people together. The terror of what might go wrong was why she got into the PR business in the first place. *We are so different and yet the same*, Freya thought. *We both love a good disaster.* The difference was that Jules excelled at fixing them, while Freya just blew everything up and then disappeared into the jungle.

Freya heard the gasps and felt the energy of the room shift as the audience took in the new image. Her heart beat at a clip similar to the fight-or-flight response she often felt in the jungle. The image behind her was that of the United States' Ambassador to the United Nations and former senator, John Haley. In the image, Haley had a deviant smile and clutched a hunting rifle. His other hand lay claim to the severed tusk of a rhinoceros. It was a side of Haley few knew about, and those who did were silenced. The beloved ambassador was known throughout the world for his empathy and progressiveness, as well as his devout Christian faith. He was the constant moderate liberals would deign to march with and conservatives would welcome to Sunday dinner.

Until now.

A sudden shift occurred in the center of the auditorium. Freya nodded to Gemma once more, and before Jules could snatch the laptop from her, a second spotlight clicked on. It was Haley. His team was urging him to stand. The ashen-faced ambassador stared at the image. Hushed murmurs turned to gasps as the celebrated humanitarian and honorary guest speaker for the event rushed through the aisle toward the exit. The spotlight followed him.

"I think you all know this face," Freya said. "We're celebrating your humanitarian efforts this evening, aren't we, ambassador?"

Haley turned and smiled mid-aisle. The color returned to his face as he acknowledged Freya with his familiar, toothy grin. "Dr. Blue, I took part in no such activity. I think we can all agree that this image has been doctored." Haley, the popular frontrunner for the upcoming presidential election, was urged on by his team.

"I can assure you, Ambassador Haley. This photo wasn't doctored. In fact, it was taken by your colleague and the current United States Vice President, Dean Craft."

A second image flashed behind Freya. It was a similar scene, but depicted Haley and Craft holding a casual conversation in front of the dead rhino. Gasps could be heard from the audience as Haley's measured personality transformed to one of anger, and he exited the auditorium. Members of the audience documented the man's shocking change in character with their smart phones. Once he'd left the scene, the audience's focus shifted back to Freya.

"I'm not here to point fingers. I'm here to protect the animals of my home. Ambassador Haley isn't alone. As you can see, the sitting Vice President of the United States took part in this hunt. Haley is one of a growing number of politicians who publicly swear to defend places like the Democratic Republic of the Congo. Yet, in private, they hunt nearly extinct animals. These representatives sit on the boards of environmental non-profits, one of which hosted this event. Haley is not an anomaly. So, all I ask of you is this: Question your elected officials. Dig deeper. We all have skeletons in our closet. But which skeletons are we willing to live with if we want our homes and environments to survive? The rhino in this image is nearly extinct. Its tusks sell for hundreds of thousands on the black market. Haley and Craft paid for trackers to lead them into the jungle and kill it. Is that who you want representing you? For those of you who are here to listen to my discussion on the endangered animals of the Congo, you can find the entire lecture on the website of Virunga National Park, my home." The website address flashed over the image of Ambassador Haley and Vice President Craft.

"Thank you, and please continue your fights for our land and animals. It makes a difference." Freya released her iron grip from the lectern and felt the blood return to her white knuckles. The audience sat in stunned silence as she left the stage.

She wondered how many enemies she'd made. *It's okay. I'll deal with it later.*

2

~

Jules Blue never wanted kids. It seemed to her, after their mother passed, she was the only Blue family member with their amygdala fully intact. She took on the role of caretaker to her daydreamer of a father, Howard and her sister, Freya, whom she considered the wildest and most untended child in the world.

As an adult, Jules quickly realized that the life she'd carved out for herself was still that of a caretaker, albeit a well-paid one. She opened up shop as a PR expert to the hapless, filthy rich one percent who often blew up their lives in the public eye. Instead of making dinner for her exhausted father or hunting down her wild sister, she reinvented A-list celebrities with sordid addictions and helped conservative politicians gain followers through tearful television confessions of dysfunction and a desperate desire to 'do the work.'

Correcting the rise and fall of notable people was an addiction; a fact she reluctantly admitted to her counselor and then denied in subsequent sessions. She had the power to make or break people with questionable values and practices. Lately the desire to muck up their personas was palpable. At the end of the day ninety percent of her clientele were terrible human beings.

It just so happened that her own sister had now become one of the troubled ones. Freya took the parts of her life that were settled and easy and bashed them against a tree until they shattered. As a powerless teenager, Jules felt superior when Freya blew it. Now, well into adulthood, she found herself praying that her sister would stop driving her life about like a bumper car. The Hague event was Freya's chance to reinvent herself, attract a younger audience, and speak from a more meaningful platform.

Jules had squeezed every one of her political connections to get Freya in the spotlight she so deserved. There was something remarkable to Jules about how Freya remained in the Congo, carrying on the arduous work of their father. She deserved recognition. Jules and their other sister, Chidi, desperately wanted to see Freya move on to bigger things before she crossed the precipice of middle age and stopped trying, or worse—sank into depression and the bottle, like their father. The possibility was high, given Freya's recent downward spiral after splitting from Logan, her husband of fifteen years.

Signs of the split were apparent when Logan took a work assignment two continents away. It was the first crack in a deep friendship and love that had kept Freya on the straight and narrow for most of her young adult life. The two were inseparable since Freya met him on summer break from Oxford. Without Logan, she acted like an unmoored boat with a penchant for bashing up against a rocky shore.

Jules recalled Howard on his deathbed, slurring missives

into Logan's ear while Freya hacked at bamboo in the backyard with a machete. *Hold tight to Freya. Your bond goes back lifetimes. One's heart beats a bit slower without the other, you see.* Logan had held his hand and lifted the flask of gin to his lips when Chidi wasn't looking. Logan turned out to be the son Howard never knew he wanted.

When Jules was nervous, which was rare, her fingers tapped against her body at a ridiculous pace. She'd learned, from years of kickboxing classes, not only that she liked to hit things to relieve stress, but how to calm the fight-or-flight response. The tick-tick-tick of her heart sped up and matched the movement of her fingers. Had there been a punching bag nearby, she would've gone to town.

Jules and her assistant, Gemma, stood on the sidelines as Freya walked to the podium. She'd forced the longtime field researcher to practice walking around her flat in the Manolos she'd lent her for the event. Jules recalled the audible exhale she'd emitted as she watched her sister clumsily make her way around the flat. She'd instantly ordered Thai, another self-preservation tactic.

Despite the pre-lecture jitters, Freya was doing well. She could turn it on in the moment and act like a woman, even if it was all fake. Jules had taken the bottle of wine away from her early the previous night. *Fucking Howard*, Jules thought to herself. It was easier to blame their father for everything that went wrong in life, especially when he was dead and couldn't defend himself.

Jules noted Gemma's breath rising as Freya stepped to the podium. The earnest assistant had come to her from her alma mater, Cambridge. Jules was loyal to three things in her life: her family, her clients, and her beloved Cambridge. She'd plucked the young woman right from graduation, having recognized her strong bent toward problem solving and technology. She had an engineer's mind, while Jules moved in broad strokes. Jules could picture the solution to the problem; Gemma assembled the step-by-step instructions so she could get there.

The young assistant looked up at Jules and smiled awkwardly, then returned her gaze to Freya. They'd run through the event five times back at the office and once onstage before the audience filed in. But for some reason, beads of perspiration lined the usually unflappable young woman's forehead. *She must not like the pressure of public situations*, Jules thought. *Hmm... she'll get used to it.*

Jules' focus returned to Freya, who stood at the podium, frozen. Jules counted the seconds in her head. Since she and Logan had separated, Freya delved deep into her research, becoming somewhat of a recluse. The invitation to speak at The Hague was a once-in-a-lifetime and career-defining opportunity that would hopefully also serve to revive her sister. *Come on. Come on, say something. Say something now.*

It was then that Freya turned and glanced at Gemma. Without acknowledging Jules, Gemma typed something into her laptop, and the next moment, all Jules could hear were gasps from the audience.

Jules' jaw dropped and the fight or flight kicked in. Her gaze flitted from the podium to a guilty-looking Gemma, who stared straight on, her face ashen.

"What is this... what's happening?"

Gemma looked like she might be sick. "Freya asked me—"

"She asked you what?" Jules whispered, frantic. "What? I told you not to listen to my sister. She's been hanging about monkeys too long."

"We have to save them." Gemma's face looked pained as

she glanced at the image behind Freya, the one that was causing the audience to pull out their phones.

Jules had been solely focused on Freya until she saw the image they'd posted. "Aww… no… no, you bloody idiot."

There she was, blowing it all up. Just like she had when they were kids. Always getting them into scrapes or trouble with their father. Jules had always been the fixer until she'd learned, at far too young an age, that Howard was flat-out unreliable. It's hard when you realize that your parents aren't superheroes; that they're not right about everything; that the people you put on pedestals are just people—fallible people who make huge mistakes.

Jules was laser focused on Freya's next move. Otto, the Hague's event director, was storming toward her. She found herself manhandling Gemma, pushing her toward the backstage. "Get Davies. Now."

Gemma had set down her laptop moments before and was seemingly prepared for Jules to strangle her. "Dominic Davies?"

"What other Davies do you think I'm talking about? Get him on standby. He'll go on in two minutes."

"But… he has security… and, and handlers."

It was true that getting the Deputy Prime Minister to speak at a moment's notice was a great challenge.

"Say the words 'Cambridge study sessions with Jules.'" Jules heard Freya's voice in the background, but she was forced to face Otto's wrath. "And if you say those words to anyone else—"

"You will end me," Gemma said, before darting around Otto and running off.

"Make her stop," Otto whispered, frantic. He looked like a child whose doll had been taken away. "Make it stop now. You told me she was talking about extinction!"

Freya was leaving the stage. Jules finally drew a breath when she saw a ruffled Dominic Davies preparing to take her place. He flashed her a pained smile and waved. Gemma stood behind him as his assistant straightened his tie and a makeup artist dusted the sheen off of his perspiring brow. Gemma gave a thumbs up and an announcer interrupted the audience's stunned silence to announce that Davies would be speaking. Sparse clapping could be heard as he walked to the podium and flashed his megawatt smile.

Freya joined her sister in the wings and Jules recalled that feeling when they were kids just before she would smack her across the skull. But this time, Freya hadn't taken away one of her toys. She hadn't insulted a boyfriend. She'd accused a U.S. Presidential hopeful, the moderate Republican and supposed activist, John Haley, of being a prize hunter.

The aftermath would be devastating. Despite the altruistic nature of her intent, this would end badly on a public scale for Freya. She would be lucky to ever work again. Haley had ties to every international political outlet and most environmental associations. *People forget*, Jules was known to say to her clients. *And in those moments where they themselves are horrible people, they tend to forgive.* In other words, Haley would survive this episode and live to see another day. After all, he was a man—a white man. White men still ruled the world. But there would be a reckoning for Freya. Decades of study and published works would be overshadowed by the public's view: that of a washed-up, middle-aged researcher—and a woman at that.

As Davies delivered one of his usual stale lectures, Jules was able to calm the frantic Otto, who had done her a great favor by booking Freya as a headliner. *Spin. Spin it.* This was when Jules was at her best. She could convince the world that the blue pill was really green and that they should take the blue pill; that bad people were actually great people.

Otto's expression shifted to one of gratitude. She pointed to the white-collared Davies, who was onstage and speaking, desperate to keep their sweaty Cambridge nights a dark secret; the ones where he was courting Jules and his future wife at the same time. Jules had discovered his double dealing and chucked him immediately. He'd cheated the wrong woman. Payback would be a life sentence.

Jules was taken out of her reverie by Freya squeezing her hand. This was code for '*get me out of here.*' Freya hated the spotlight. She only lectured for the benefit of the animals she loved so dearly. Jules wrapped up with Otto and dragged Freya through hallways of gawkers, some clamoring for a picture or an autograph from the now-infamous woman who had singlehandedly, if only temporarily, hampered Haley's dreams of building a Camelot of the South and potentially, his presidential bid.

~

3

Freya felt her body finally exhale as the side stage shielded her from the audience's gaze. A stark realization hit her. *It's over*. Or was a new phase of life just beginning; one where she fully inhabited the feeling of being an outsider, rejected from a pack she'd never belonged to in the first place? She'd felt her pulse rise as she'd nodded to Gemma. The decision to move forward with her plan was made in a split-second. She'd written a list of pros and cons, and, despite the cons quickly overtaking the pros, decided to move forward with outing Haley. Now that it was over, she felt the disappointing fall, the inevitable dealing with repercussions.

In convincing herself to out Haley, she assumed that most people had the same empathy for sentient beings that ruled her own value system. She imagined she would simply escape into the jungle and allow Jules to band-aid her image, for whatever it was worth. What Jules hadn't been able to instill in her yet was that most people were awful, and it was the stark minority that was preventing civilization from falling into complete depravity. *Look to history,* Jules had said. *Outright cruelty is just no longer a part of the social contract. But rest assured, women are placed on tiny stakes every day to die a slower death. At least Joan got it over with in one go.*

Jules gave her the look. That of a disappointed mother; the same look she'd given her back in the DRC when Jules had gotten them out of trouble with their teachers, Kinshasa authorities, but especially with their father, who was easy to convince because he was usually drunk. She would spin stories until Howard remembered the past incorrectly, just so they wouldn't get grounded. Freya called it the Blue Sickness; the determination to win an insurmountable situation. It was a condition their oddball father had instilled in them from the time they were young. As little girls, he dragged them into the jungle, desperate to bond with a specific pack of gorillas, likely drunk the whole time.

Otto turned to Freya, irate. "Haley was the keynote speaker!" He turned to Jules. "Does she even realize? What were you thinking in bringing her to me? I have an hour of live programming to fill."

Jules was in her element; the sickness firmly taking over. "Freya is a rule-breaker, Otto. You knew that when you booked her."

"You pushed her on me," Otto said. "You pushed and pushed... and now my career is over!"

"No, darling, it's not." Jules placed her arm around Otto and led him away from the stage. Freya was urged into motion by Jules' free hand yanking her along. "Otto, this is just the beginning. It's you who put the dull World Environmental Forum on the map. Do you realize the hits you're getting right now? Darling, you'll be getting a promotion before I'm through singing your praises."

Otto glanced at her, confused. "What is this?"

Gemma shoved her phone in his face to show him the social media focusing on the event.

"Otto, you booked the 'it' girl of the environmental revolution," Jules said, wrapping her arm over his shoulder and guiding him to the hallway. "She's here to make a difference. Take a stand against infamy. And you were instrumental in that."

"She was supposed to speak for an hour!" Otto said. "Now I have an audience sitting there, and there's her hour and Haley's hour to fill... I don't understand how you think this is a good thing."

"Darling!" Jules said, laughing, pointing at Davies. "See? It's taken care of!"

Otto glanced at the stage where Dominic Davies had stepped in.

"All part of the grand plan, darling Otto. Your name will go down in history, and it's the *right* side of history. Now get to work. You can thank me later."

After considering Jules' opinion, a flustered Otto embraced her and gave her a fervent kiss on each cheek. "I'll see you at cocktails later."

"Of course, darling," Jules said, waving goodbye as he stalked off.

"It's an absolute marvel to watch you work," Freya said.

Jules' face darkened as she turned to Freya and Gemma. She grabbed Freya by the shoulder. "You, come with me. And you... clean this up," she said to Gemma, who nodded and clutched her laptop to her chest.

Jules ushered Freya along, gripping her wrist and

pulling her through the gathering fans. "Thank you! Freya's on her way to another event. Thank you."

Once the fanbase thinned, Jules unleashed on her in a pained whisper, through a clenched smile. "What in the bloody hell were you thinking?"

"I just... it seemed right. It felt right."

Jules stopped and pulled Freya into a nearby utility closet. "Felt right? Don't you usually jump before you think? Since when do you stop to assess feelings? Don't forget what Papa always said."

"Feelings get you killed," Freya said.

"Because if you stopped and used logic, you would've determined that outing a bloody presidential hopeful was career suicide! All you had to do was give a bloody lecture. Not tip the whole Hague on its arse!"

"Then he shouldn't have tracked and shot a nearly extinct animal!"

Jules rubbed her brow. "I've got the CIA, the Republican National Convention spokespeople, the New Yorker and all of this... blowing up my phone!"

Freya dared to place a palm on Jules' back. "Come on, sis. You love a good challenge."

Jules' expression remained dark, and Freya quickly glanced around them to make sure there weren't any weapons available for Jules to pummel her.

Instead, Jules screamed into a bag of laundered linens. "Total Freya! Act and think about it later. Jules will clean it up. Well, this time you may have not only screwed your own career, but mine as well."

"You'll just have to come and live with me in the jungle."

"Never will you ever—"

"See me in that cesspool of a jungle again," Freya said,

cutting Jules off. "Yes, yes, we know. And we still love you. Miracle."

"I have central air conditioning and heating. I don't own a fly swatter, because any bugs that dare enter my penthouse are sucked into my ventilation system. I have a ventilation system. You most definitely do not."

"But you don't have any gorillas to cuddle with," Freya said. "What is life without—"

"I have a portrait of dear Binta hanging in my office. I say goodnight to him every night. I don't need monkeys."

"Poor you." Freya smirked.

"You just... you don't get the gravitas of what you've done. Not only to Haley. But to yourself." Jules took a deep breath, exhaled, and opened the door to the utility closet to find a group of reporters clamoring for a word. They called out Freya's name and Jules ushered her past them.

4

~

Everything in Jules' sight screamed luxury; the dresses, the sheen from the polished grand piano, the crystal chandelier above the ballroom table. Jules spotted the glazed look of relief on lecturers' faces; that of having accomplished a lofty goal in front of noted colleagues and competitors. Jules overheard some party-goers conversations—they were still buzzing about Haley's fallout and speedy exit from the event.

A notable story had found its way through the thin cracks of her PR facade that delved into the deep dysfunction of her family. It was something she hadn't experienced. The drama had always caused others pain, not her own sister. Jules felt bad for Freya, who had always been a fool, but a fool with a good heart. She would jump off a cliff if it meant saving one more rhinoceros or lion or her beloved gorillas.

Jules found her name on the placard and set her purse down at her seat. She noticed water stains on her knife and set it on the tray of a passing waiter, in trade for a glass of champagne. Your sister is *a perpetual toddler. You don't have to save her.* It was true. For as long as she could remember, Jules attempted to buffer Freya's haphazard life from danger, while she bounced from disaster to disaster, miraculously coming out on top each time. *But not this time*, Jules thought. *People love to watch others fail so they can feel better about their mundane lives.*

Work the room. Her internal voice reminded her of a life coach spouting out -isms for her to follow. *This is an opportunity. Introduce yourself. Find the troubled ones and get some new clients. Win-win.* Too much therapy.

Jules sipped the champagne. She wanted to sit in her disappointment for a moment. She tapped her salad fork against the tablecloth to stop from checking emails, texts, the constant barrage of information that might distract her from her mission. She was there to flout the positives of Freya's presentation. She was reminded of the gauche word art her team had given her as a joke five birthdays ago: *Believe in the best of people, even if you don't want to.*

To their shock and surprise, Jules hung the missive in her office, kitty-corner from her Jasper Johns. It was sacrilege, but she loved it. Aside from the psychopaths, whom she avoided, people were usually some combination of awful and stupid; they simply needed an education in how to be decent human beings.

Jules loved the existential challenge of her work. *How can you teach someone to be good? How does one manipulate another's first impression?* It was her chosen art form—to mold society's thoughts until they became popular opinion. Conservatives were easy to sway because they liked things to stay the same, as long as it didn't affect their net worth. *Tell them once and they'll take it as gospel.* Questioning required too much effort to change. The liberal left, however, were more skeptical. So it was all about repetition without faltering. *Tell them enough times, and they start to doubt themselves. Tell them enough times, and they will follow you to the ends of the earth.*

Jules was counting the taps of her fork against the pristine tablecloth when she should have been working the room. She was there in place of Freya, who promised to remain in hiding until the scandal blew over. She started to think about strategy. How could Jules begin to repair her sister's reputation, and by extension—her own? Being related to a radical may have been hip in the big city circles when they were younger, but now, firmly in middle age, Freya looked like an impatient schoolgirl blowing her mouth off at the playground.

Jules' thoughts swayed from one end to the other. Freya was holding the Senator accountable and shedding light on the inhumane poaching industry. But outing someone in a venue of peers was often unforgivable, an act that would create enemies the world over, and destroy the inroads Freya had been making in the DRC. She leaned back and closed her eyes, the tapping against the tablecloth increasing.

A second glass of champagne was set before her, and her free hand grasped for it. In a moment of thoughtlessness Jules said, "Thank you," without bothering to address the waiter.

"It seemed like you needed a drink for both hands. Your spare one is beating the tablecloth to smithereens."

Jules' lips curled into a smile as she caught the accent. Spanish, likely from the Barcelona region. She'd heard this one before.

"I have not once seen the great Jules Blue alone at a party."

Jules turned and nearly choked on her sip of champagne. "So, you're leaving your world-famous diamond company to go into catering? How original."

Hugo Lacort, heir apparent to the Lacort gem fortune and newly named CEO of the company itself, stood before her. He had spoken at the conference that very day, though Jules had missed it due to the fallout from Freya's big performance. Not only had he lifted his father's reputable business into the 21st century, but he had also reinvented the diamond mining industry to maintain more ethical and modern standards. Only days after his father's passing, Hugo announced the change along with outing his competitor's unethical mining practices in Africa and establishing a trust for victims of the industry.

Experts and his shareholders said it was a quick death march to the end of his father's legacy, but Lacort's stock prices shot through the roof. Hugo became a voice for the families that had been victimized by unethical mining practices. Lacort's image grew, and so did his humanitarian voice on the international stage. In person, Jules found herself overcome by his riveting features.

"I'm quite surprised you don't have an army of handlers around you," Jules said.

"I prefer to keep things simple." Lacort's gaze circled the room, catching every stare that clocked where he was and who he was with. "People who have other people do everything for them are helpless at the end of the day. Wouldn't you agree?" His eyes finally landed on her, consuming every detail of her face, her bosom, her thighs.

"You are the most interesting person in the room, Jules Blue."

Jules laughed. "Oh, am I?"

He placed his hand on hers and smiled. "I want to hear your dirtiest stories."

Jules leaned in, the champagne taking effect. She never crossed the line with prospects, but welcomed the flirtation after one of the roughest days of her life. "Do you want to know, Mr. Lacort, why I'm paid so very much?"

He smirked as his hand slowly made its way to her thigh. "Oh yes. Please tell me."

"Because I can keep a secret."

Hugo laughed. "This is probably the best conference I've attended all year. I expected to drink my way through boring discussions with stuffy scientists, but this... this is a surprise."

The back of his hand brushed her thigh and Jules' worries were replaced by the fresh flirtation.

"I bet you've had a hard day admonishing your sister," Hugo said, his face close to hers.

Jules sipped the champagne, wanting to forget about Freya. It tasted better now that she was flirting with a handsome man. "Funny you say that, because I have banished her to the tower. The Queen will order the beheading shortly. I'll save you a front-row seat."

Hugo laughed and flagged a waiter. "Excuse me, sir. The lady needs something stronger. Two '64 Dalmores, please."

"You must really want to make me feel better," Jules said.

Hugo held out his hand. "I have been waiting many years for the opportunity."

Jules blushed and took his hand.

"I'm so glad you left your naughty sister at home so we could enjoy this beautiful evening. Shall we walk?"

The waiter delivered the two Dalmores. Hugo took her champagne glass and replaced it with the scotch. The brown liquor warmed her throat. She felt her shoulders relax as she and Hugo walked out onto the verandah. Maybe it was the Spanish accent, but she found herself forgetting about work, about the day she'd had, about Freya.

"The Hague has kindly reserved the library for my discussions this evening," Hugo said. "Perhaps we can retire there to talk?"

"Discussions?" Jules snapped out of her reverie. *This is business. He's here to talk about Freya's speech.* "Of course. Yes."

The same waiter appeared, gathered their glasses on a tray, and led them to the grand library. He opened the two massive wooden doors to the library and Hugo guided her in. Wall-to-ceiling first editions graced the shelves surrounding the glowing fireplace. The city lights of The Hague shone through the windows; the measured layout of the city spanning before them in precise grids.

Fuzzy warmth covered Jules, and she suspected it wasn't just from the fire. The scotch was doing its work. She was all business all the time. For once, she wanted to let it all go and take in the attention from a man she so admired. "I should get back in there," Jules said, giggling like a schoolgirl. "You're not the only client I'm courting, you know. Besides, I should work on restoring my sister's tarnished reputation."

"Should," Hugo said. "That word was uttered to me so many times as a child. It has become meaningless. You shouldn't do anything you don't want to do." He looked at her and smiled. "I have known about you for so many years. When you were petitioning for the Lacort account years ago, I encouraged my father to hire you. We languished for so very long under his... ancient reputation."

"Your father was a force to be reckoned with," Jules said. "He knew the diamond business better than any other. I'm so very sorry for your loss." Emiliano Lacort was known for lifting the diamond industry into the marketing behemoth it was today. Lacort diamonds were synonymous with everything high end and beautiful. Far out of reach for most people, Hugo was determined to make Lacort diamonds accessible to a whole new segment of customers.

"Thank you," Hugo said. "I have an idea. Why don't we work together now?"

Jules straightened up. *This was a professional meeting*, fact confirmed.

Hugo smiled. "What happened? Your whole body just tensed."

"I... am trying to remain professional." Jules laughed. "You're making it difficult."

Hugo leaned in and kissed her neck. "I'm sure the great Jules Blue can handle mixing a little business with pleasure." His lips traveled to hers.

Though Jules had never entertained a client's advances before, she found herself giving in. A minute later, her head was spinning, and not from Hugo's attentions. She pressed herself up on the couch; her gown askew and her vision fuzzy. "I'm feeling poorly all of a sudden."

"Oh?" Hugo said, watching Jules as she stood. "That's a shame."

Jules faltered, and she sat again. In moments like these, she could only see Howard in the back of her mind, spouting off his usual fatherly advice. *When in doubt, disguise yourselves in green leaves, climb a tree, and if that doesn't work, run! Run, Jules. Run for your life!*

"I shouldn't have mixed..." The first editions circled her vision until she was finally able to focus on Hugo's face. He didn't seem troubled at all.

Hugo helped her relax against the couch pillows. “Maybe the wine was off.”

A niggling feeling overcame Jules as she recognized Hugo’s look; the vacant, sociopathic kind she’d spotted in various horrible clients over the years. “The scotch. What did you…?”

Hugo glanced at the waiter, who entered the room, then back to Jules. “Nothing gets past you, does it? Oh, don’t worry. It’s just a little something to relax you. And you really do need to relax, Jules. I can feel the… tension from a mile away.” Hugo’s lips curled into a wicked smile.

Jules felt her body go numb. “What have you given me? Help!”

Hugo covered her mouth. “No, no, none of that. You just made it… so easy. I was expecting more of a challenge. I’m sort of disappointed, to be honest.”

The waiter approached them as Jules’ vision went fuzzy. Hugo leaned in and caught her before she passed out. “We’re going on a little trip. To your beloved Congo. But, don’t worry. Nothing will happen to you. Unless Freya makes… another bad decision.”

“Freya… “ Jules struggled as the drug washed over her until everything faded to black.

5

~

The ancient heater in The Hague hotel room that Freya and Jules shared clicked on and off throughout the night. Immediately after the debacle, Jules had installed Freya in the room and told her not to leave or read any news or social media. Freya did all she could to avoid the wave of emotions she was feeling. They ranged from a faltering sense of pride to utter humiliation. She worked on a research paper. She watched old movies. She took a long bath and ordered room service. *He was a bad man*, she repeated to herself. If only she'd been there when he was about to take his shot. It wasn't just a rhino he'd taken out, but her potential offspring that might help remove the species from the endangered animals list. *It was my duty to take him down, one way or another.* Despite her early years as a member of the Black Adders, the Verunga anti-poaching unit, this was a different way of taking down a poacher. The Adders operated in shadows and darkness from a set of laws they'd invented for themselves. In taking down Haley, Freya had made a unilateral decision that would likely take her down with him.

She tried sleeping, but only stared at the ceiling. She considered options for her future. Was there a future? *Focus on the work like you've always done.* That meant heading back to the DRC, her beloved homeland, for research. She could still get that kind of work, even with a tarnished reputation. *The jungle is honest, at least.* But the lectures, the publishing career, the university positions? She could kiss those goodbye.

Against her better judgement, she logged on to her computer. After reviewing the emails from her publisher, her agent, even some old colleagues, Freya felt defeated. Scathing admonitions of the night's actions, a hard-won career obliterated in the matter of a few PowerPoint slides. *Think about the repercussions of your actions*, her agent had said in a voicemail, before slamming the phone down. She took a sleeping pill and waited for it to take effect.

Freya fell asleep pondering a lifetime of admonishment that reminded her she'd never really left pubescence. *You could've gotten yourself killed. What were you thinking?* But the impulses of her body moved faster than the wheels of her brain. She'd been in fight or flight as long as she could remember.

Her eyelids shut, heavy with sleep. She longed for the warmth of the Congo and pulled the duvet over her body. Jules would forgive her by morning, surely. They would hug and depart to different parts of the globe, and Jules would set to work piecing together what was left of her reputation.

6

~

Still heavy with the effects of the sleeping pill, Freya fumbled for the alarm and hit the snooze button. She sat up and switched on the light as the previous day's events flooded back to her. The desire to be back in Virunga, hidden from the world by the jungle canopy, hit her as she threw her suitcase on the bed and packed haphazardly. She stopped and walked to Jules' connecting room.

She knocked on Jules' door. "Time to get up, sleepyhead. I've got my flight of shame to catch."

There was no response. She knocked again, before opening the door. "Hey. Jules?" Freya switched on the light. The bed was untouched. Jules hadn't sent any messages, so she called Jules' mobile. Straight to voicemail. Maybe she met someone? She sent a message. *Check in with me, will you? I want to make sure you're okay*. Freya dropped her phone on the bed and jumped in the shower. She was drying her hair when she got out, and realized it was still early. *Give it a bit. She's probably asleep in some attractive man's bed.*

Freya packed up her things and stared at her phone. Ione, Jules' London assistant would be in the office any minute now. She would know what was up. She pulled her hoodie over her head, afraid of running into anyone who attended the debacle from the day before. She wheeled her suitcase to the front desk and checked her phone, before locating some coffee. She sat down and dialed Jules' office.

A familiar voice answered. "Blue Marketing. This is Ione, how may I help you?"

"Ione, it's Freya."

"Well, if it isn't my hero!"

Freya smirked. "I'm glad I still have one friend."

"Things are darkest before the light, Freya. That's what Jules always tells me. Just avoid socials. But don't worry! We're working on a strategy, because it's pretty... bleak."

"Socials?"

"Yeah. Just don... you know what?" Ione caught herself. "Never mind what I say. It's all bollocks. How may I help you this fine morning?"

Freya was not one to be concerned about social media, but now she felt the need to check the accounts Jules' team had created for her. She clutched her coffee mug and remembered what she'd called about.

"Have you heard from Jules? She went to this..."

"Embassy dinner, right? She checked in last night. Sent an email around eleven pm asking about... Oh, Hugo Lacort."

The name was familiar. "Lacort diamonds." The coffee was bitter. Or maybe it was that Freya had a general loathing for diamond miners. They were parasites . Lacort claimed to be more ethical than his father, but she hadn't seen the generosity benefit the communities around her.

"Yep. She asked for background and references."

"Hmm, she never came home last night. We're supposed to go to the airport together."

There was silence on the other end. "Hmm... well, he's quite an attractive chap. Who could blame her?" Ione's voice trailed off in a chuckle. "Listen, I have worked with Jules for ten years. The woman knows how to handle herself. My guess is she'll be on the next flight out."

"But she would've checked in with me," Freya said. "We had a plan."

"Listen," Ione said. "It's none of my business, but when Jules is upset, she tends to avoid. You know?"

"Right, right." Classic Jules. Silent treatment until one pays the appropriate emotional debt. "I apologized over and over yesterday."

"Give her a minute, Freya. She knows she has to deal with PR nightmares with her clients. I think she was looking forward to seeing you, and..."

"And I messed up."

"She wanted to spend time with her sister, you know, watch your star rise and all, and it turned into work," Ione said. "Again, none of my business, but she's probably pissed. She'll come around."

Freya clutched her mug tighter. Guests were starting to filter into the buffet area. She yanked her hoodie over her forehead. "Everything you're saying makes complete sense. I'm the twat. Jules is perfect, all is right with the world."

"No, you're not. You're her sister, and she wants good things for you. I'll tell you what. You get on your flight, and I will hunt her down. You'll have a text from me by the time you land. I'm quite sure of it."

"Thank you, Ione," Freya said. "You've put my mind at ease. Do me a favor. Send me the information you forwarded to Jules about Hugo, will you?"

"Oh, sneaky sister," Ione said. "I will, but you mustn't tell Jules."

"Of course not." Freya smiled and hung up the phone. She sipped her coffee and thought of one more thing. Chidi, her other sister, would be awake by now. Maybe she'd heard from Jules.

About to board my plane, Freya texted. *You will pick me up, right? I land at 11:15am in Kinshasa. By the way, heard from Jules? She didn't come home last night.*

Text bubbles appeared as Chidi was responding. *Way to take down a future president of the free world, sis! Yes, I am planning on picking you up. Haven't heard from J. We both know she's avoiding you. Ha!*

Freya smiled. At least one of her sisters was still talking to her. She collected her suitcase from the front desk and sent Jules one last text before departing.

I know you're mad, but please check in with me, so I know you're okay. Freya stepped into her car as the driver placed her suitcase in the trunk. A couple waiting nearby stared at her and whispered as her car left for the airport. She pulled her hoodie down and closed her eyes. Maybe she could get some much-needed sleep on the long flight ahead of her. She would hear from Jules by the time she landed.

7

~

When Hugo Lacort closed his eyes he didn't see darkness. He didn't envision the few private moments with his mother that he'd cherished before she was taken from him, or the faded memories of a little brother he was too young to save. What he saw was the diamond in all its glory. This vision began appearing after his father passed away, and it was as though Emiliano's obsession with Isolde's lost treasure had somehow transferred to him. Sure, he'd heard the stories of the curse that came along with the diamond, but he was willing to suffer the consequences of holding the diamond versus being plagued by its image for the rest of his life. He knew each of its angles, its perfect cuts; the gleaming perfection of a thing of nature carved for the purpose of pleasing one person. He knew passing facts about Isolde, the Congolese queen who had bucked the trend after her husband died and ruled in his stead versus marrying again. He fixated on Isolde's diamond and wondered if he was actually seeking her spirit to inhabit him in all its defiant glory, and not the thing itself. It clouded his vision until he awoke with a panful migraine. If there was such a thing as a curse, he was afflicted by it.

Hugo glanced out the window of his plane. They were in hour ten of their nineteen hour flight. Jules would wake in the country of her birth. She was a wrinkle in his plan; a nuisance that changed the trajectory of his expectations. He sipped a cocktail and closed his eyes. He hated last-minute changes. Half the world seemed to operate from a spastic, reactionary way of behaving that adversely affected the other half. He believed that the pain of the world—war-based land-grabs, lost love, terminal sickness, could all be eradicated through careful planning and organization. It wasn't a surprise that his plans to transport Freya Blue from The Hague back to her Congo homeland had been foiled by Freya herself. Apparently she was one of these people who operated on fluctuating realities. He wondered how she'd made it so far in life. It was her fault that Jules was dragged into this. *And why am I trusting Freya Blue with my plan?* Hugo thought. *Because she's the only one I can.*

He took the deep breaths he'd been trained to by the specialists he'd spent thousands on. *When things don't go your way, stop. Take deep breaths. Feel the breath reach every corner of your body.* They all wanted him to focus on his breath. But his mind never stopped. All he could focus on was how his plans were going awry, and how he could reach his goals more efficiently. Whoever wasn't onboard would get left behind or die. He expected this outcome for the Blue sisters, but they were small sacrifices in exchange for the remedy of holding Isolde's diamond.

Hugo caught a glance at the bound Jules Blue as the attendant entered her cabin. *Freya had to go and blow up the world*, Hugo thought. *Now all eyes will be on her.* And as a result, Hugo would be pulled into her whirlwind of risk. When Freya didn't turn up at The Hague dinner, he was forced to take Jules in her stead. It was a haphazard plan, the execution of which made his skin crawl. The woman was connected to every PR firm in the world, not to mention politicians, world leaders, and members of the secret service. Her absence would be noted. But she would quickly understand that it was in her best interest to remain silent. The woman was nicknamed *the lock and key*. She'd never revealed her clients' secrets, even when pressed by MI6. If Jules cared about Freya and her other sister, Chidi, she wouldn't start talking now.

Chidi, on the other hand, was always a part of his plan. The quiet scientist. She wouldn't put up a fight. It would've been a simple trek into the jungle, led by Freya, one of the very few who could navigate to the volcano while managing the risks associated with its inhabitants. That was until Freya pissed off the fanatic right.

There was a commotion in the back of the plane as Jules awoke, dazed. Hugo heard her cries from his seat.

"Where am I?" she said. "Where are you taking me?"

Hugo's two guards held her down while his doctor for hire gave her more sedative, this time through an IV. The door was shut, and the stunned flight attendant walked over and shakily offered Hugo a glass of champagne. Throughout the long plane ride, he'd lost his performative patience. He swiped the champagne from her tray and glanced out the window before watching her nearly stumble back to her seat and sit down. Her eye line fell to her lap. Hugo was sure she was wondering how she would make it through the next nine hours of the flight.

That's when he felt the familiar rage boil up. He closed his eyes and tried to breathe as his vision went black and he felt the tension rise in his muscles. When he got like this, his vision of the diamond faded away in flashing white sparks. He opened his eyes again, and his hands balled into fists. He stood and walked to where the flight attendant was sitting. He grabbed her by the collar and yanked her to her feet. She started screaming, and he dragged her over to his second in charge, Javier.

"I ask one simple thing of you. Find me loyal team members who understand the assignment."

Javier remained coolheaded, as though he'd seen this type of outburst before. "She signed an NDA. She won't talk, I can assure you."

"This is the wrong kind of person." He dragged her to the back of the plane and down the stairs to the lower level. In the back of his mind, he thought he could hear the echo of her screams, of her pleading for her life, but he couldn't make sense of it. His vision burned red as he dragged her down a flight of stairs. The modern interior of the cargo plane's upper level gave way to the rugged lower level, manned by Joseph, one of Hugo's team of Congolese specialists.

He waved to Joseph, who stood at attention, stunned.

"Open the door!" Hugo yelled.

"Sir, we're mid-air. I think you should. She can sit here with us, if—"

The attendant screamed.

"Open the door or you'll join her." Hugo's vision narrowed, his temple burned, as he heard Javier in the background begging him to reconsider.

The attendant's screams intensified as the back door of the C-130 lowered. They were blown backwards by the gust of air, and Hugo inched his way toward the door. He pushed the woman toward Joseph.

"She's ready to disembark," Hugo said. "Why don't you help her?"

Joseph paused, stunned, before quickly outfitting the flight attendant with a parachute. He then walked her as close as he could to the edge of the door. He placed the pull cord in her hand.

"Count to ten and pull this," Joseph said.

The attendant sobbed, pleading with Joseph to help her. Hugo stormed towards them, and with a swift kick, she was sucked out of the airplane. Hugo grasped the side of the plane and felt a massive release as his rage reached its apex. He closed his eyes and pulled himself back inside. He regained his footing as the door closed, and the vision of the diamond returned.

He could breathe again. He opened his eyes and saw Joseph and Javier staring from a distance, shock painted on their faces. He straightened his jacket and brushed past them. Though he didn't want to admit it, it was becoming more and more difficult to separate his public persona from his private one. He felt his rage spilling over into the everyday. The unfortunate side effect was the occasional loss of life, but he was no stranger to it. His father had done worse. It was just their bad fortune to find themselves in his presence when he lost himself.

Hugo returned to his seat, and Javier approached him.

"Do you want the doctor to see you?" he asked. "He can give you something... if you need to calm your nerves."

"Get me a drink," Hugo responded. "And let's hope, for your sake, the rest of this excursion goes to plan. Or you will be launched next."

Javier spun around and walked to the minibar, where the flight attendant sat only moments before. Hugo watched as he mixed a drink, stalked back, and handed it to him.

Javier walked back to his computer and pretended to type, though his hands were shaky. Hugo wiped his brow. *I can't afford to lose any more help today.*

"I'm sorry," Hugo said. "The travels are getting to me."

Javier turned and nodded. "Of course, boss. We're almost there. And everything is taken care of. Don't you worry."

Hugo had stopped apologizing for the deaths of those around him after Emiliano had died. It was the mention of her name, the mere passing of his mother's name from Emiliano's lips, that had sent Hugo into his first rage. He wasn't about to say her name, not after what he did to her and Eduardo. It wasn't his right to mention the only two people Hugo had ever loved; the people who had been ripped from Hugo's life at Emiliano's hand. He'd wondered, at the time, how Emiliano came to enjoy cruelty. But as he held the man's neck between his hands and squeezed that night just a few years prior, he understood that the same rage coursed through his veins. His mother and brother were too gentle to survive such typhoons of anger.

The moment Emiliano took his last breath was the moment his obsession with the diamond had transferred to Hugo. Emiliano's limp body lay atop scattered pages that contained sketches of the diamond and its probable location. Still engulfed in his rage, Hugo had pushed his father's body aside, and laid his eyes upon the only thing Emiliano had ever truly loved; Isolde's diamond. He would have it. He would have what his father could never claim as his own.

8

~

Freya exited the airport and a balmy gust of air hit her. She squinted in the blinding sunlight. It was a vastly different tone from the somber blues and grays of the Netherlands and a vastly different energy. Kinshasa citizens moved in quick bursts: to collect luggage and leave; to call out each other's names; to take over a spot on the thoroughfare that another car may have been angling for. The result was a chaotic jumble of weathered yellow and baby blue compact cars intermingled with the occasional Rolls Royce or Mercedes Benz.

Freya's mobile phone buzzed with incoming messages as she stepped onto the bustling sidewalk. Car horns honked, their drivers frantically waving at the passengers they were picking up. Freya ripped off her hoodie and felt her skin warm in the afternoon sun. It was chaos, but she was closer to home. It made her forget the maelstrom she'd caused until she saw the local papers. Her image was painted across each one. *Congo daughter ousts next President. Is Freya Blue a hero of the jungle? Or enemy number one?*

Freya ran her fingers through her mussed hair, rubbed her eyes, and pulled the hoodie on again. She stood in the middle of the airport lounge as passengers filtered out of the plane and passed her. She poured through messages.

Three messages were from Ione. *I know you're probably on the plane, but call me if you can. Sorry, Freya, I wouldn't text again, but please do call. Okay, you're in flight.*

One came from a stranger. *Dr. Blue. My name is Dr. Remy Nkosi. I have been referred to you by Ione at your sister's PR company. Please do call me at your earliest convenience. I must talk with you.*

Her phone rang. It was Ione. Freya answered immediately. "Ione? What's going on? I've just landed."

There was a big sigh from the other end. "Thank god. It's you. Jules still hasn't contacted me. I received some concerning information from one of the sources. A Dr... "

"Nkosi. I've just received a text from him." Random people started to recognize Freya and point her out. She walked along the arrivals sidewalk, hoping to avoid any interaction. Chidi would be there shortly.

"All the other sources were positive. But his was... I think you should speak with him."

Freya's heart started pounding. "Call Chidi. If he's in the diamond industry, she might know him. I'm going to hang up and call Dr. Nkosi."

"Right," Ione said.

Freya paced as the airport crew disembarked around her. *Where was Chidi? She was always early.* The dial tone rang as the pilot nodded her cap to Freya and smiled.

"Hello?"

Freya started at the sound of the voice on the other end.

He sounded South African, familiar. "Dr. Nkosi? This is Freya Blue. I think I recognize your voice somehow."

"Yes, Ms. Blue. Please call me Remy. You may have heard my podcast. I'm also interviewed quite a bit. Jules handles my PR. I'm glad you contacted me."

Freya glanced around her. No Chidi in sight. "You know something about Hugo Lacort? My sister was likely with him last night, and she hasn't been in touch."

A sigh from the other end. "Please keep this in confidence. I am putting myself at risk. I know Jules and was instantly concerned for her when her assistant reached out."

"What is it?"

"I wish I could forget my time working for Hugo Lacort and his company. He is... unsound. I know that I sound like a disgruntled employee, but I can assure you, that's not the case. He is... a deranged individual.

"Is Jules in trouble?"

"If she's with him? She'd be safer in a lion's den at night."

Freya felt foggy. She sat down as a cleaning crew passed her by, picking up garbage from the street.

"You must get her away from him at all costs," Remy said.

"I can't reach her. The last I saw of her was before dinner last night... at The Hague."

"Well, you must find her. I'm going to forward Graham Watson's info. He's in intelligence... he might know something. And Freya? I'm on a burner. I can't be traced. Even though I'm a public figure, I fear being found out by Hugo. Just so you're aware of the weightiness of this situation. Read the email I sent. And get Jules to safety as soon as you can. I will be in touch."

Dr. Nkosi hung up and Freya immediately dialed Jules'

mobile. Straight to voicemail again. She called Chidi. The line rang for ages until her voicemail finally picked up. "I'm home. I'm guessing you're en route back to London. See you soon." Freya hung up and searched her email for Dr. Nkosi's message. She scanned her messages again and found a message from an unknown sender with no subject—likely Dr. Nkosi. She stopped to contact Ione.

"Freya," Ione said. "Any news?"

"Do you know a Graham Watson?"

The line went silent, and Ione cleared her throat. "Erm... how do you know that name?"

"Can we reach him?"

"Jules would never allow it," Ione practically whispered.

"We have no choice. Jules is in trouble. Tell him the situation and see if he can help. Chidi is picking me up at Kinshasa."

"I couldn't get a hold of Chidi," Ione said.

"Nor I. She loses mobile service driving down the base of the mountain. Ione, will you do what I asked?"

"Jules will kill me, but... have you read Nkosi's email?"

"I'm about to."

"Just remember, when you read it, we know nothing. Don't make assumptions. That's what Jules always tells me."

"Not making assumptions got her in this mess." Freya sighed and rubbed her brow. "That, and me acting like a complete and utter child."

"You're a hero," Ione said. "Everyone knows it. Haley is abhorrent."

"Tell that to Jules when she surfaces. Let me know what you find out from Graham, will you?"

She ended the call and realized that she had somehow made it to baggage claim. She opened the message from Dr. Nkosi.

Bags rolled by, and Freya read the message.

I worked for Emiliano and Hugo Lacort for eight years, researching the mining situation in South Africa. What I saw was a horror that I will never forget. Emiliano hired me to research ways to frack the delicate surface of our region. I was charmed by Francisco and Hugo. Outwardly, as to many, they seemed the utmost gentlemen and professionals. As I continued to conduct my research, I became more ingrained in their daily lives. Emiliano was an obsessive workhorse. He worked night and day, trying to understand how he could expand the company. During my research, he moved me into a wing of their house to protect the secrecy of the project. What I witnessed was a nightmare that plagues me to this day.

Emiliano was abusive to everyone around him, but especially to Hugo and his little brother, Eduardo. Eduardo died in a boating accident around the age of 8. It was said that he accidentally drowned, but a very young Hugo was never the same after it. I suspect Emiliano caused the death. Their mother passed not long after trying to escape the Lacort compound with Hugo in tow. A guard shot her in the middle of the night, right in front of Hugo. It was horrible. Hugo was left only with his monster of a father and a lifetime of grief—at a very young age.

I was around Hugo when he was a teen, during those delicate, formative years when a boy is becoming a man. Emiliano openly beat him in front of the housekeepers and staff. I tried to intervene on one occasion, and Emiliano hit me and threatened my career. We all kept our mouths shut for fear of retaliation. And I'm afraid that Hugo has turned out the same.

Freya stood staring at the conveyor belt while the last remaining passenger gathered his bag. Freya's suitcase spun away from her as she played back Dr. Nkosi's message in her head. Her phone buzzed, and she quickly grabbed her suitcase from the conveyor belt.

It was Chidi.

Drama at the lab. I sent Alfred to pick you up. Sorry.

"Alfred?" Freya said. Alfred was a local farmer the Blues had been friendly with since childhood. They rarely saw him outside of the occasional walk near his farm. He never drove to the city, let alone out of the lowlands. Something was off.

Freya searched her bag for sunglasses. She'd become accustomed to the Hague's constant grey skies. It was then that she noticed Alfred sitting in his old truck, waving with hesitation. She rolled her suitcase toward his car and realized that he wasn't getting out of the truck, which was odd. He was a man of extreme manners, yet both of his hands remained on the steering wheel.

She smiled and leaned in through the window. "Hey stranger. How about a ride?"

Alfred, usually the first to crack a joke, had a brow covered in sweat. He forced a smile and nodded nervously, yet both hands remained on the wheel.

"Alfred, I'm so sorry that you had to drive all this way to pick me up. I could have hired a driver."

"It's no worry," Alfred said. "Chidi said to tell you she's sorry. She got caught up at the lab." He checked the rearview mirror repeatedly as Freya climbed into the passenger seat.

"So I heard," Freya said, getting into the cab. "Thank you for picking me up in her stead. I know that this is a very long trek for you."

Alfred checked his blind side, indicated, and merged into the chaotic Kinshasa traffic. "Of course. Of course."

"Alfred, are you alright?" Freya asked. "Want me to drive? I get it, you know. City driving can be a stress."

"No... no. I will drive." Alfred accelerated at a snail's

pace, while car horns honked all around him. He nearly jumped in his seat.

Freya clutched the handle of her carry-on bag. She hated polite conversation more than anything, and it was a long drive back to the lowlands. She'd been hoping to talk to Chidi about Jules' situation. That was what they did when they picked each other up; chatted about the third sister, who wasn't in the room. She braced herself for the long drive and pulled out her phone. Dr. Nkosi's email was still open. She archived it and closed her inbox.

As they approached the lowlands, Alfred accelerated. They sat in an awkward silence as swampland gave way to the green of the jungle basin. Freya leaned her head out of the window and breathed in the warm afternoon air, which smelled fresher once they'd left the city. Despite not knowing Jules' whereabouts, it was a comfort to be home.

"You, you shouldn't do that," Alfred said. "This... is an old car. That window and door aren't very stable."

"Just getting some fresh air."

They were entering the rural lowlands, which gave way to the old dirt roads Freya was used to. The truck slowed to a near stop as Alfred pulled onto a side road.

Freya gave Alfred an odd look. "Why are we stopping here?"

They were mere meters from Chidi's lab. Before Freya could respond, a figure rose in her periphery from the back of the cab and held the butt of a gun to Alfred's head.

Alfred gave Freya one last pained look. "Run."

Before she could scream, a shot was fired and Alfred slumped over the steering wheel with blood pouring down his temple. The last thing Freya remembered was reaching for the door handle just before she felt the cloth cover her mouth.

9

Freya woke to the familiar view of Chidi's grassy yard. Exotic birds and animals scattered into the brush only to reemerge moments later in a gust of dirt. She inhaled the misty morning air and saw the native orchids that littered Chidi's garden. She pressed her temples as she recalled the evening before and felt the beginning of a throbbing tension headache. Her vision came to as Chidi entered the room and smiled.

"What happened?"

"You're okay. Just take a minute," Chidi said. "I'm not sure what they did to make you pass out, but it must've been some kind of chemical. You don't have any contusions."

"They?" Freya's eyes focused, and the background came into view. Behind Chidi appeared two armed men, followed by a well-dressed man in a suit, uncharacteristic dress for the Congo. She recognized his face from the litany of press he'd received at the conference. Hugo Lacort. His penetrating gaze focused on her, and she felt the psychotic madness disguised by the well-respected reputation. *Dr. Nkosi's warnings.* Freya pushed herself up and winced in pain.

"No," Chidi said. "You need to rest."

Freya disregarded Chidi and stood, slowly approaching Hugo. "What have you done with Jules?"

"Nice to meet you as well, Dr. Blue." Hugo wasn't ruffled by Freya's approach. "Jules is just fine." The wicked look Nkosi hinted at appeared. "All of you will be fine if you cooperate. You see, this was actually your doing. Jules wasn't supposed to be involved at all. Yes, we needed a little help from Chidinma here—she was always a part of our plan. But your little stunt yesterday at The Hague threw everything into disarray. We acted quickly and brought Jules along with us. So putting her life on the line is... on you, I'm afraid. And getting her back is up to you as well."

Freya stopped in her tracks, considering the past day's events. "Alfred. You... you killed Alfred."

Chidi covered her mouth and turned to Hugo and his men in shock. "Oh, my god."

"What is it you want?" Freya asked.

"Start by understanding that there is no one else in the world that can give me what I want. You know the mountain... the Mikeno volcano better than anyone," Hugo said. "You will lead me to it."

"The volcano?"

"You killed Alfred for... " Chidi sighed, then turned to Freya. "He's a treasure hunter."

Freya winced. Alfred murdered for an old fairytale. "What could *you* possibly need with treasure?"

Hugo smiled. "So you know who I am. That's good. Then you will understand what I'm after."

"It's a myth," Freya said. "It's an old wives' tale mothers

tell their children so they don't go wandering into the jungle."

Chidi squeezed her hand, urging Freya not to prod him. "Where is our sister? Where is Jules?"

"The treasure exists," Hugo said. "My father hunted it for most of his life. He found proof. I am here to finish his work."

Freya closed her eyes at the thought. "Do you know how many people die making the Mikeno trek every year? Not to mention, it's illegal to go past the park barriers. You'll attract attention."

"You've come the closest, Hugo said. "And survived. You will take us there and help us find the treasure."

"People are already looking for me," Freya said. "They're asking for interviews about The Hague event. They'll find you, eventually."

Hugo leaned in and nearly whispered in Freya's ear. "I've taken care of that story on your behalf." He showed her the headlines on his phone. *Shamed researcher goes into hiding. The black history of the unstable researcher, Freya Blue.*

"Of course, if you cooperate, we can spin it the other way too. Jules can help us," Hugo said. "You can get everything you want. Acclaim for your work. Stopping a known trophy hunter from taking the presidency. Together, we can flip these headlines. Freya Blue resurfaces, triumphant. Freya Blue was right about Haley all along, sources say. I'm sure your sister can get you a Pulitzer. All you have to do is get me to the treasure."

"What happens when you get there and there is no treasure?" Chidi asked. "Do you kill us then?"

"My father wouldn't spend his every waking hour up until his death craving something that wasn't real," Hugo said. At the mere mention of the diamond, the gleam of madness appeared in his eyes.

"It's a sickness, don't you see?" Chidi said. "You're not the first to obsess over it." She paused. "It's part of the curse."

Hugo pointed at Chidi. "You believe it's there too." He looked to Freya for recognition. "You have to acknowledge that it's real."

"It's real to every Congolese child who is told the lore from the second they take a breath."

All Freya could think about was how her last-minute actions put Jules at risk. Her head was spinning. "Where is she?"

"She's safe. Help us find the treasure and we will release her. That means we make it out with the treasure and return home safely. You act disagreeably and... you won't ever see her again. Fair trade?"

"You won't survive," Freya said.

"You did. And you will again."

"She made it to the base of the volcano when she was a teenager," Chidi said. "On a stupid dare. She was also evacuated by Medivac. She was in hospital for a month."

"But she survived," Hugo said. "That makes her the only person in the entire world who can get us there. Rumor has it that Howard Blue made it even further. You're like cats with nine lives. Survival must be in your blood."

Chidi rubbed her eyes in frustration and turned away. "Fucking treasure hunters."

"I want to see her," Freya said. "I need proof that she's alive."

Chidi faced her. "You can't seriously be considering this."

"What choice do I have?" Freya asked.

Chidi turned to Hugo. "Don't make me choose between

my sisters. You know nothing about this jungle," Chidi said. "The stories... "

Hugo laughed and rolled his eyes. "You mean the curse." He stepped closer to Chidi. "My father believed in spells and goblins and curses, too. It's foolish lore told to scare off those who seek the treasure."

"It's not witchcraft that kills you in the Congo," Freya said. "The best trackers in the world can't teach survival skills. It's a death march."

"Here are the facts: I don't believe in witchcraft, and Freya Blue made it up the side of the Mikeno Volcano. That's all I need to know," Hugo said.

"Whether you believe in Isolde or not, the jungle doesn't like it when things are taken from her," Chidi said. "You take from her, she takes from you."

"I think you've been living here a bit too long." Hugo broke into laughter and spun his fingers in circles, indicating that Chidi was insane.

"Do you know anything about Isolde?" Chidi asked.

"What do I need to know about a dead queen?" Hugo asked.

Freya closed her eyes. "Chidi will have you know that she's very much alive."

"A long time ago, the Congo was ruled by opposing royal families that constantly warred over land rights," Chidi said. "Years passed, and the greediest members of the families mysteriously died off, all in horrific style. Great kings went mad from their desire for the land that they couldn't claim as their own, so much so that two of them dove to their deaths over jungle cliffs. It was said that the kings, at the time of their death, were in some kind of trance."

"A surviving queen of one of the families, Isolde, hoarded the jewels of the families that had died out. She was said to be buried alive at the age of twenty-eight. Her nine-year-old daughter was found beside her, holding her mother's hand—"

"While her other hand gripped a massive diamond," Hugo said, cutting Chidi off. "I know the story. I want that diamond."

"Treasure hunters traipse through the park grounds every spring," Freya said. "If they return at all, it's always in a body bag.

"Lead me to the treasure and we'll see about that," Hugo said. "Choose not to go, and all three of the Blue sisters die out, anyway. It's up to you."

Freya sat up and felt her feet touch the cold floor. She stood and approached Hugo, but Javier blocked her from getting too close. "I want regular check-ins to prove that Jules and Chidi are alive. We leave at dusk. And if anything happens to either of my sisters, I can assure you, it won't be the jungle that kills you." Freya pushed Javier aside and left the room, feeling as though she'd signed her own death warrant either way.

10

Chidi stalked into the back yard to get some air. She closed her eyes to the familiar humidity and comforting birdsong that enveloped the night. Parrots soared overhead, scattering canopy branches before diving into the depths of the jungle. For a second she was alone, considering her options, wondering if she could possibly make a run for it and tell the authorities. But Hugo's temperament was unstable. She couldn't risk what might happen to her sisters.

She wiped away the gathering beads of perspiration from her face and noticed Hugo's Congolese guard approaching. His name was Albert. At first she thought he'd said "Alfred," and was immediately heartsick and furious, thinking about how Hugo had killed her friend without a second thought. Hugo had tasked him with keeping a close eye on her, and his constant shadow was almost more unnerving than the fact that he was armed. More of Hugo's guards continued to filter in after Freya woke, all appearing to be of Congolese or British descent. Hugo had surely laid the foundations for his treasure hunt well in advance. A British guard named Will traipsed behind Albert, this one with a dead look in his eye, as though holding people captive was what got him out of bed in the morning.

Chidi turned to Albert, speaking in their native French.

"It takes two of you to keep me in check?"

Albert rolled his eyes and looked away. Something told her he was reluctantly assigned to this post. It was one thing to hold an upper-class white woman accountable. It was plain shameful to take down a fellow Congolese. And Chidi wasn't going to let him forget it.

"You really want to follow this idiot into the cursed jungle? Isolde knows, and she will haunt you and your family for all time. Didn't your mother teach you anything?"

Albert shifted. Mere mention of curses and witchcraft made the locals uncomfortable. *"The government made that story up to keep people out of the jungle, so they can mine it. It's common knowledge."*

"What about your children... your family?" Chidi asked. "*Do you ever want to see them again? You know if you do this, you know you won't.*"

"What's she sayin'?" Will waved his gun at her. "Enough chat. Time to go inside."

"I need some air," Chidi said.

"It wasn't a question," Will said. "Move. Now."

"Don't be difficult," Albert said. *"It will be bad for your sisters."*

"What you sayin' to her?" Will tapped Albert with the edge of his automatic rifle.

"It's fine," Albert said, pushing the rifle away.

"Then speak in English," Will replied.

Chidi turned away, frustrated, and headed toward the lab. If she was going to be Hugo's bargaining chip, she would demand some freedom of movement.

Will trained his aim on Chidi and laughed. "You think they'll miss this one? There's three of them, right? An heir, a spare, and..."

"If she is harmed, her sister will not help us," Albert said.

Will laughed and refocused his aim on Chidi's back. "I think she ran, and we didn't have a choice."

Chidi glanced behind her but kept walking. Will's face had become animated at the threat of killing her. She'd been in this position before. Most Congolese women had. Better to die swiftly versus being raped or tortured to death. But before he could shoot, a massive figure leapt from the bushes and pinned him to the ground.

Chidi whipped around before seeing him and whispered, "Binta."

Albert backed away as the four-hundred-pound gorilla descended on Will and tore into his cheek. Will's body convulsed as Binta bit into his face again until his screams were replaced by blood sputtering from his mouth and neck. Albert struggled to cock his gun before Binta's attention turned to him. Binta stepped on Will's gored face as blood sputtered out beneath him. Chidi heard nothing but Binta's guttural growl as he focused on Albert and bared his teeth. Albert cried out and backed away. Binta rose up and stepped toward him.

"Set your gun on the ground very slowly," Chidi said.

Albert shakily lowered his gun to the ground, crying for his life. Binta stalked toward him, the fur on his face matted with Will's blood. Chidi glanced at the distant lights of the compound. They were far enough away from the main house that no one would likely have heard Binta's attack. She could let Binta finish the job, then run for help. *But Freya and Jules.*

Binta pinned Albert's arm as he stood over him and bared his teeth.

"Brother," Chidi said.

At the sound of Chidi's voice, the gorilla was awakened, as if from a trance. He glanced at her with a rediscovered innocence, as his hand pinned the whimpering Albert to the ground. Chidi stepped toward them and carefully moved Albert's gun away.

"Sit next to me," Chidi said, signing the words. "This is Albert. He promises to be nice now."

Binta looked curiously at Albert, then back to Chidi, before releasing his hand and stalking towards her. He sat next to her as she took in his blood-covered face. It was odd seeing Binta this way. She knew he would do anything to protect her, but it was shocking to see him turn into something other than the calm creature who padded around the compound all day, nibbling on bamboo.

Albert sat up and caught his breath as a much calmer gorilla sat before him.

"I have to get into my lab," Chidi said to Albert. *"If I don't send a message to my colleagues in Kinshasa, they will know that something is wrong. They expect my reports daily."*

Albert started inching toward his gun, but Chidi shook her head and moved it away with her foot.

"I will play your game for the sake of my sisters," Chidi said. *"But I need to go to my lab. And if anything happens to us, my brother will kill you, too. Do you want that?"*

Albert whimpered at the thought. *"N... no. But... Hugo will expect us back."*

Chidi considered their options before turning to Binta and wiping his brow.

"Go to the hiding place. Stay there," Chidi signed with bloodstained fingers. *"I will come for you."*

"Chidi come now," Binta signed. *"With Binta."* He grunted anxiously and pulled her hand toward him.

"I must stay. Freya needs me."

Binta perked up at the thought of Freya.

Chidi grasped the gorilla's hand in hers. *"Not safe. There are guns here."*

Binta was the Blue family's brother. The loyal silverback gorilla had been raised by Howard Blue after being abandoned by his pack as an infant. From the start, Howard raised Binta and Chidi with sign language. Freya and Jules, having only known Howard's parenting style as haphazard at best, dubbed them *Howard's favorites.* The three went everywhere together, and it appeared to them that Howard didn't want to 'muck up this time around.' When Howard died, Binta trained his affections on all three sisters, and he was often seen around Chidi's lab or Freya's jungle cottage. Howard didn't have many rules, but he was strict about them steering clear of areas where gunshots were heard, most often a sign of poachers. Binta would listen.

Tears collected in Binta's eyes. He grabbed Chidi's hand and dragged her along with him, but she pulled him back.

"No," Chidi signed. *"You go alone and wait for me. We will be together soon."*

Binta embraced her and backed away before disappearing into the brush. She turned to Albert, who exhaled and fell to the ground. He grabbed his rifle and shakily aimed it at her.

"My lab," Chidi said, defiant. *"One whistle and he will come back for you."*

He studied her for a minute before lowering his rifle. *"Quickly, then."*

Chidi stopped before they entered and pointed to the cameras located in every corner of the room. *"Stay at the entrance. The camera feed goes straight to my company headquarters."*

"Any messages you send will be scrutinized," Albert said.

"Tell Hugo that this is normal procedure," Chidi responded. *"It will attract attention if I don't check in."*

Albert rubbed his face and lifted a radio to his lips. *"Nothing happening here. She wanted to check on her lab."*

A voice crackled over the radio. "Understood. Proceed."

"Remember," he said. *"If you send for help, there will be consequences."*

Chidi nodded. After signing on to her computer, she composed an email and tagged a colleague in Kinshasa to review the daily log. Her hands started shaking as she blind cc'd a recipient she hadn't spoken to in years.

Thanks for checking the log, Grace. I hope you have a great day! Shutting down for the weekend and taking the day on Monday. Also, our cousin is going to the county fair. We hope to see you there too!

Best,

Chidi

Chidi hoped that Grace, an analyst to the core, would see the message, shake off the odd comment, and review the log. Scientists searched for raw facts, but Chidi wasn't known for bungling communication. She was counting on the long-lost recipient seeing the message, too.

She logged off of her computer and shut down the systems entirely, which might flag a warning to her

Kinshasa team. Plus, Chidi rarely took days off. Grace might send someone to check on her. But by then she and her sisters might be dead.

She met Albert at the door. *"All done."* He pointed the butt of his gun toward the house. Chidi could only hope she hadn't endangered anyone with her risky move.

11

Jules knew she was back in the Congo when she felt the heavy wet heat brush against her skin. Her view was obscured by a blindfold, but she felt the bright afternoon sun and heard the unmistakable bustling and horns of the busy Kinshasa streets surrounding her. The drugs they'd given her made everything feel heavy; the mere act of separating her lips to speak felt impossible.

How did she get here? Freya was the risk-taker of the family. Jules liked her schedule, her creature comforts, and the safety of a well-padded bank account. And then it came back to her. *Freya. The Hague. Hugo.*

The afternoon light suddenly went black, and she felt her body being moved, as though she was going underground. The city street sounds became muffled until she heard nothing but the constant drip from a faucet. She was being hidden away somewhere by Hugo's men, it seemed.

Jules swore she'd never set foot in the Congo again after Howard had passed. Life had other plans for her. She felt her lips form words, but they sounded slurred when they came out.

"I can pay you more," she heard herself say, as her wrists and ankles were tied to a chair. "Let me go. I will pay you double what he's paying."

She wasn't sure that what she was saying made any sense to Hugo's men, because all she got in return was a swift slap across the face. The pain slowly burned through her cheek and eye, to her nose. She then felt the guards administer more drugs, and her head went slack. Questions filled her mind before she passed out. *How can Hugo seem so charming? Is Freya alive, or is she as good as dead, too?*

12

Toner Residence, Palo Alto, California

Logan McLean's time was no longer his own. The mobile phone buzzed and jumped along the coffee table. Maybe he needed to pivot to something boring, like insurance. These bratty tech CEOs clung to him like flies on cow dung. Most days he wanted to throttle Sascha Toner, but the idea of prison was only slightly less desirable than the contract he'd been talked into at the lowest point in his life.

Palo Alto's current it-boy and full-time neurotic had politicians and lobbyists on speed dial, a firm place on Forbes' billionaire list, and a team of handlers that curated his public persona to that of a demigod. He also, Logan painfully discovered, had limited social skills and an irrational desire to buck the system, such as when he hacked into the U.S. government's mainframe as a teen and scored jail time.

Logan interviewed right after he and Freya broke up,

mainly just to get Sascha's handlers off his back. Visibly hungover during the call, he quoted an ungodly sum to accept the job. At the time he didn't care about his business or reputation; only about drinking good whiskey and his one-way ticket to Thailand. Sascha Toner changed all that.

The TONDON CEO, who'd said very little during the interview, was miraculously impressed with Logan. He accepted the ridiculous terms, jettisoning the former SEAL's plans to float around the Hong Islands for six months. Toner, Logan was told, expected the best of everything from life, including his security detail. Previously, when Logan's life wasn't in shambles, he headed up Palo Alto's most well-respected and utilized security company. But after going through a year-long separation from the one woman he drank with for years and the one woman he had to drink to forget about, Logan started phoning it in.

The simple solution was setting up Sascha with his team of well-trained guards. Who wouldn't say yes to that kind of paycheck while checking in weekly from Phi Phi. But Sascha threw more money at the problem until he finally agreed to be his point man. *Sascha gets what Sascha wants*, was all they could say. *No number is too high.*

Logan hadn't visualized his career taking this path. Still, he couldn't complain; he normally ran the company while assigning the task of babysitting grown men with zero glamour and oodles of money to his team. He was used to globetrotting and putting out fires from a mountaintop in the Alps or a beach in Bali. Nowadays, he kept Sascha safe while pondering daily the amount of money that actually made one happy. *Is the money worth it when you feel like you're chained?*

The phone buzzed again. Sascha, of course. Logan rubbed his eyes and unlocked his phone. Twelve texts. *I need you. Hello? Okay, seriously, come here now. Emergency! I think I've made a mistake here. Need your input. Where are you?*

A salmon twilight shone on the manicured garden as Logan trudged up the path to the main house. He flashed a key card, let himself in through the back entrance, and stood at the base of the stairs, arms crossed in defiance. "This better be important."

Sascha appeared at the top of the midcentury staircase, dressed in a navy robe and matching slippers. "You've been here this entire time?"

A female voice sounded over the in-house intercom; Sascha's smart system, designed to help him when a human assistant wasn't there. It said, "The blue shirt matches your eyes."

Sascha sighed, gazing at the ceiling. "My eyes are fucking hazel! Who programmed you?"

Logan chuckled and rubbed his eyes. *How did I get here?*

"Oh, it's funny, is it?" Sascha asked.

Logan wiped a tear away. "I don't know if I should laugh or cry, man." He looked at Sascha with renewed sincerity. "Yes, Sascha. It was funny."

Sascha grunted in frustration and stormed into his bedroom.

"Come on, Sascha!" Logan dragged himself up the stairs.

"It's time to decompress," the smart system said. "Start with a deep breath."

Logan entered Sascha's bedroom to find him in his vast walk-in closet, inhaling deeply.

"I'm sorry," Logan said. "What security needs can I help you with?"

"I've been texting you for an hour." Sascha turned and stared at the identical, meticulously hung suits and shirts.

"What's the emergency?"

The voice sounded over the intercom, "The next best choice is the grey. Studies show that more jejune tones evoke trust."

"Grey makes me sad, but maybe pewter... nah, forget it." Sascha ran the tips of his fingers along the suits until he was on the opposite side of the room from Logan.

Out of sheer habit and a sudden itch to move, Logan started a set of up pull-ups in Sascha's doorway.

Sascha took Logan in and solemnly placed a hand on his belly. "There's a gym for that. That's very distracting. For all genders, regardless of sexual preference."

Logan dropped to the floor. "I'm done for the day. The night team will be checking in any minute. What do you need?"

"You know, you're turning into a very... " Sascha's gaze turned away from Logan as he considered his words.

"A very what?"

"Unlikeable... "

"Did you hire me to be likable? You have the best security in town."

"You could just... give a little—"

"What do you want?"

"I don't... I don't know which one." Sascha waved a hand across the expanse of his closet. Hangers full of black, grey, and white t-shirts, matching suits, and Italian leather shoes lined the rows.

Logan pressed past him and quickly picked out a navy suit, brown loafers, and a crisp white shirt. "You've been in Palo Alto too long, man. You gotta start wiping your own butt again."

Sascha's public persona was carefully guarded, so much so that he'd become dependent on the handlers who lovingly scheduled board meetings and interviews so that he had time to decompress and guarded his privacy at all costs. His outward face to the world was whip smart, controlled, logical. But behind closed doors, Sascha was everything but. He soon came to see a brilliant grown man with the emotional quotient of a teenager.

"Oh, it's the date tonight, isn't it?" Logan asked.

Sascha paced, kicking the shoes he'd chosen for himself out of his way. "It's just... so much one-on-one time."

"That's generally what happens—"

"And I'll be thinking about how I'm sweating the whole time and I won't be able to focus on... on her." Sascha stared at the ceiling and cracked his knuckles.

The smart system chimed in. "Sweating suggests a healthy genome, which the female sex finds attractive in a mate. Fight or flight syndrome indicates a healthy response to threats."

Logan dropped the clothes on the wardrobe island. "Get dressed. Wear deodorant. Suggest a cocktail to start. Ask her about her life."

Sascha nodded. "You're the only one I feel like I can talk to. No one tells me to wipe my butt anymore. Not even my mom."

"So, wipe it, Sascha. And who knows? Maybe this woman will capture your heart by not telling you what you want to hear."

"We both know that's not going to happen."

"Then don't settle until you find a woman with her own mind." Logan said. "I'm leaving now."

"She's a supermodel, Logan. You know Evan from Snapchat, his wife hooked it up, and... I can't meet women otherwise. I can't go on an app like every other schmuck. I can't date women at my office."

"Why not? Bill Gates did, and he's happily married."

"Was. And she took half. And why'd you have to go and bring up that tool?" Sascha picked up the suit and started getting dressed. "He would've been me too'd in this day and age, and you know it."

"If you can't show all of this... what's going on here... to your girl," Logan motioned in Sascha's general direction. "... then you shouldn't date her."

Sascha stood, his shoulders hanging dejectedly. "Let's face it. Women like... what... you've got going on. They only like my bank account and my name."

"If you believe that's the case, then treat this as a practice date. You need to be away from all your... people for a minute, and just be around a normal human being, you know?"

"Practice... on a supermodel?"

"Maybe you'll be surprised."

Sascha nodded and straightened his suit in the mirror. "We had a somewhat nice telephone conversation once I got around the Slovakian accent."

"And this?" Logan pointed to the cell phone. "For emergencies. Only." Logan backed out and hightailed it out of Sascha's room before the conversation could continue. He thought he heard Sascha calling out to him, but he pretended to play dumb and kept walking.

~

13

Back in the guest house, Logan poured himself a glass of Hakushu '18. His entertainment of late was patrolling the dark web chat room, *McQueen's Place*, mostly filled with former team members' reminiscences, as well as references to current missions and their whereabouts. Logan was the first to admit that he frequently suffered from insomnia and alcoholism and a serious case of FOMO. Staying looped in made him feel alive.

He couldn't help but scan through current missions, a habit that raised his blood pressure. There was nothing like the rush of energy he got from leaving everything behind and jumping on a plane to go to an undisclosed location. The thrill of never knowing what might happen next, who you might run into, or whether you might live or die was a feeling he couldn't release.

An email preview caught his eye. *Chidi...?* His estranged sister-in-law, emailing from the DRC. Though he was still legally married to her sister, Freya, they'd split the year prior. Freya called it "geographically irreconcilable differences." Logan's business and Freya's lectures took them all over the world, but usually away from each other. And when they were together, they sank into their drinking so much that they didn't recognize each other anymore. Soon, life and its temptations pushed them even further apart.

Thanks for checking the log, Grace. I hope you have a great day! Shutting down for the weekend and taking the day on Monday. Also, our cousin is going to the county fair. We hope to see you there too!

Best,

Chidi

County fair. Logan sighed. Freya and Chidi were child guards of the Black Adders, sworn to protect the jungle and its inhabitants for life. County fair was their radio code for when things had gone too far. Maybe they'd run into a nasty poacher they couldn't handle. Whatever the specifics, the county fair meant that they needed help. The way she concealed the meaning meant that Chidi was also under duress.

Logan ignored the texts from Sascha that were pouring in. He turned on his security feed and relocated the signal to Freya's house in the DRC. Usually, a pulsing blob of light emanated from Freya's lone cottage in the jungle. But tonight there was no light. There was no power at all. He scanned the lower basin to find that other homes on the same grid had power. His instincts flared.

He lay back on the couch and took a sip of his drink. "She's not your problem anymore, Logan." He stared at the ceiling as the all too familiar idea of entering a dangerous circumstance pulsed through his veins. It took him years of therapy to admit that he was addicted to the thrill of danger, as Freya never would. *Addicted to the possibility of death*, the analyst told him. Two people attracted by their affinity for adventure; bouncing through the world together and courting death.

He sat up and stared at the black light, signaling that power was off at the old DRC house. Then he did something he promised Freya he would never do: He hacked into her computer and checked her emails. He mulled through her "sent" file. She was a workhorse, that was for sure. Sending messages all day on Friday and Saturday, and then they stopped. He opened one with the subject line *Personnel Inquiry*.

She wanted to know about Hugo Lacort. Logan searched the name, and Hugo's image popped up. Diamond executive and heir. He then checked her inbox and found unread messages from various colleagues she'd known through her years in the DRC.

There were more recent, unopened emails regarding Lacort. *He's got a stellar PR team and seems like a mensch upon first meeting,* Maya Strevinksy wrote. *Don't be fooled. He's fucking crazy, Freya. STAY. AWAY.*

The second email was from Robert Kasongo, a fellow diamond executive of Lacort's. *Call me and let's chat about this. Can't talk about it over email.*

Logan picked up his personal phone and started calling his security team. "Sean, you around, mate? I need coverage... probably a week or two. Yeah, yeah, I'll let Sascha's handlers know. Get George and Simon to help. I have to go on a personal trip. Family related." Logan glanced at the phone Sascha had given him and turned it over and focused his gaze on Chidi's email. He hoped he could get there in time to help. "I've got some nice scotch here for your day's end. Thanks, man. I owe you." Logan quickly packed and left Sascha's phone blinking on the desk.

14

Freya closed her eyes and rubbed her temples. She breathed in the thick humidity of the night air and imagined, for a moment, that Jules was back in London, safe. Freya wished she could erase the last forty-eight hours. If only she'd behaved; acted the part of the mature researcher and given her lecture like she'd agreed to. Her head throbbed as she contemplated what was before her. Hugo continued to assert that Jules was alive and well. Freya suspected he was lying, and that Jules was already gone, all thanks to her impetuousness.

"We need proof of life before she steps foot in the jungle," Chidi said, brash and unapologetic. After a lifetime of living in the Congo, Chidi knew how to speak to war criminals; the very desperate, power-hungry leaders of tribesmen who ravaged the land and its people. They did unscrupulous things for money and money alone. Giving in to their whims and playing a victim meant rape, torture, and slow death.

Hugo was a different story. He had more money than any one person needed. He wanted something that none of them could give him: the diamond. Its lure made men sick with greed. The Blue sisters had seen it before. Howard made sure to steer his daughters clear of treasure hunters, and for good reason: treasure hunters had lost their core. Whatever values had been instilled in them, the diamond's curse had stolen long before they'd made it to the jungle. The girls would roll their eyes when he pointed out one of these hunters, but now Chidi recognized it in Hugo. Like a perverse sickness, the diamond's curse ate up one's spirit first, before it took the flesh.

Javier handed Chidi an iPad. The live video feed revealed a dank room with nothing but a harsh neon light in what looked like a basement. A figure dressed in cargo pants and a t-shirt came into view. Jules. Her head sagged, and she was bound to a chair. A hand lifted her chin to reveal her face. Jules' left eye was bruised, and she seemed barely conscious. The hand slapped her, and she momentarily regained consciousness before listlessly dropping her head again.

"You see?" Hugo said. "Alive and well."

A dark heat filled Freya's gut. She lunged at Hugo and put him in a stranglehold before Javier pulled her off and she slammed into the edge of the desk. She grabbed her side and dropped to the floor, her head spinning from the motion. She cradled her head as the throbbing headache returned.

"Do you want your sister back dead or alive?" Hugo gasped, as he caught his breath. "Alive, but maimed, maybe? That man there with her... he knows another kind of cruelty."

Javier helped Hugo to his feet.

Chidi approached Hugo, but was pushed back by his guard. "Get her food and water and unbind her now. Or you can forget your precious diamond. We're Congolese. We're not afraid of whatever death you have planned."

All attention suddenly shifted to the iPad, where Jules could be heard chuckling. Chidi grabbed it.

"He's a fucking treasure hunter?" Jules said.

"Unbind her... now!" Chidi said.

Hugo stood and dusted himself off. "You heard the lady. Get her a... better situation."

Freya fought back tears and pressed herself onto the bed. "I'm sorry, Jules... it's all my fault."

Though Jules' eye was nearly sealed shut from the blow they'd given her, Freya could recognize her stubbornness poking through in her smile.

"All you had to do was give a bloody lecture, Freya!"

Freya laughed through tears. "I know. And go to a dinner to be kidnapped by—"

"By treasure hunters," Jules said, wincing from the laughs. "Of all the fucking gin joints, you idiot!"

Hugo's delicate ego was on display. He ripped the iPad from Chidi's hand and turned to Freya. "Get yourself ready to go."

"How will I know that my sisters are safe when we're in the middle of the jungle?" Freya asked.

Hugo grinned. "Our military-grade equipment is already set up at our... shall we call this our base camp?"

"Get Jules out of there," Freya said, motioning to the dank basement. "I'm going to be asking to see her regularly. If your guards so much as give her a scratch, I will know about it."

"And if anything happens to me," Hugo began, "these guards are set to receive huge bounties for each Blue sister they kill." Hugo relented and raised his hands. "Okay, okay. Bring Jules upstairs. Some sunlight will do her good. She's an English rose, but she's… looking a bit pasty."

Jules lifted her head, clearly in pain. "Freya, I'm dead already. We both know it. Don't do this."

"Baki hai tu," Freya said. In Swahili, it meant *Stay alive.* She was betting that Hugo didn't know the language. "Sisi wote tunajua unajua jinsi ya." *We know you know how to.*

The training the three girls received at the hands of The Black Adders, the anti-poaching unit that guarded Virunga's wildlife. Though Jules had eventually turned away from the Adders to move to London, she had received the training as a teen. A slight smile crossed her lips. The kind she had when their father was chiding her for being the oddball daughter who was interested in fashion instead of primates.

Freya turned to Hugo. "It's not me you should be worried about. The jungle knows we're coming." Holding her side, she got back into bed with Chidi's help.

Hugo laughed nervously. "We leave at dawn." He stormed out, followed by Javier.

Freya lay on her side, defeated. "Bring me a map of the park."

Chidi went to the other room and came back with her well-mapped book of the park. The volcano loomed at the top. Below it, thick, unexplored jungle. Freya sat up and turned the pages, landing on a sectioned-off portion of the base of the park.

"We start here," she said.

"The back of the park?" Chidi asked. "Are you mad?"

"It's faster. By a day and a half."

"Yes, because you'll die a day and a half faster. It's forbidden, that route. Papa never let up about it. You know this."

Freya flipped the pages and traced her finger along the

intended path. "We'll put his men to work. Create a new path. May the jungle queens and kings protect us."

"You're as crazy as Isolde," Chidi said.

"You know I don't believe in the old bat," Freya said. "But if she does exist, I need her on my side."

That was the rub of Isolde. It was Congolese nature to mock her and fear her all the same. She loomed above the Congo's inhabitants from her volcano perch—waiting, just waiting for anyone who dared to trespass. No one had ever returned to tell the tale, and no one dared make the trek to retrieve the bodies of loved ones who were insane enough to attempt it.

"Of course." Chidi glanced up and mouthed *sorry* to the sky.

"You never know," Freya said. "Maybe back in the day she would've been our friend."

Chidi snickered. "We both know she reincarnated into Jules."

Freya chuckled and then was overcome by sobs. "I did this to her. I should've just gone to that bloody dinner, and then neither of you would be in this position."

"That's not true," Chidi said. "He would've used us as collateral, anyway."

"There's a million ways to die up there. I'm worried about not surviving, and then you both..." She gazed at the page featuring a painting of the volcano. It was an artist's best guess, because no one had made it that far. "Can you get our new friend, Javier, to send one of his drones up there... you know, scope out the situation? I want to see what the weather is like... what the mountain looks like... these days."

"I'll tell you what it's like. Rain, mud, clouds, rain, torrential rain. And the silverback."

"The silverback," Freya muttered under her breath.

She'd forgotten him. Isolde's ghostly guard, who, the lore had it, made quick work of any trespassers before they even scaled the volcano's edge.

Chidi checked for any guards before signing to Freya: *Our brother went to the hiding place*, Chidi signed, referencing Binta's escape. *I will send him to help you when I get the chance.* The guard standing at the door shifted as Chidi glanced up.

Oh? Freya signed.

Chidi nodded, hoping that the guard didn't know sign language. She gathered not, as he sighed and turned away. *And I'm hoping our old friend knows about the county fair*, Chidi signed. *Just hoping.*

Freya closed her eyes and sighed. Logan. Despite the rough two years between them, she missed waking up next to him. They both agreed that the separation was harder when two people loved each other so much but were simply on different paths.

I hope he makes it, Freya signed. *He's the last friend we have. Who knows? He might inherit everything.*

Yes, Chidi signed. *Everything, meaning our ramshackle cottage in the jungle.*

~

15

Logan walked toward the military plane of the private airfield just outside Palo Alto. The tiny airstrip, nicknamed the "tech vacuum," catered to the well-heeled tech executives with planes on standby, as well as the occasional military flight. It wasn't uncommon for major deals to be struck as distracted CEOs, desperate to escape the busyness of Palo Alto, jettisoned off to the Maldives, Jackson Hole, or Zermatt. Without a bubble of lawyers surrounding them, Sascha claimed, geniuses were the first to make terrible decisions.

Logan approached the plane and flashed his ID. The cargo hold was being filled with supplies and personnel; he would be the only passenger in the main cabin. Despite being worried about Freya, he was looking forward to the long flight, void of distractions. Logan's old friend had hooked him up with a military flight to Uganda, where he could easily connect to Kinshasa, and find out what was going on. He still hadn't been able to locate his estranged wife or either of her sisters, despite his connections with MI6 and the U.S.-based intelligence services.

Logan sat down and rubbed his temple. Part of him was looking forward to being back in the Congo, the place he'd called home for so long. The other part was dreading being there without Freya. He didn't know the place without her. He opened his laptop and located the surveillance on the Blue house. Not being able to reach one of the sisters was normal. Two was odd. But all three out of touch at the same time filled him with dreadful fears of what might be happening, or worse—that he was too late to stop it.

"You're going to the mother fucking Congo?"

Logan jumped at the sound of Sascha's voice as he appeared from the back of the plane like a jealous girlfriend.

Logan exhaled. "Jesus, you scare me more than your android. What in the hell are you doing?"

Sascha nursed a scotch, wavering back and forth as the plane hit some turbulence. He fell backwards, dropped his drink, and regained his balance. "I should ask the same of you! You're supposed to be protecting me."

Logan approached the cabin and waved at the steward. "I have a family emergency. Excuse me, sir. We're going to have to turn around.

"That won't be necessary, sir," Sascha said.

"You're supposed to be on a date."

"I have surveillance on you. I found out you left and I—"

"You have surveillance on me? That's impossible."

"You trained your men very, very well. But I pay more."

Logan sighed. "Sean. I'm going to fire that—" Logan turned to the Steward. "This is a very important man who needs to be in Palo Alto. There's been a mistake."

The steward shrank as Logan approached him. "I'm very sorry, sir..."

"Nope! No mistake. We're all going... where he's going." Sascha chewed on the lone ice cube reserved for his drink. "I was having a meltdown. And I couldn't find you! So Sean did some digging and here we are! Boys' trip! To the Congo... I mean, I pulled some strings, and... bought the plane, so..." He nervously munched on another piece of ice as the plane continued to the tarmac.

"You bought the... this plane?" Logan asked. "This... is a military plane."

"Yeah. Turns out everything is for sale," Sascha said, munching another piece of ice. "Especially the government."

"God dammit." Logan sat and took out a flask. "You liked playing Monopoly as a kid, I'm guessing."

"My parents always went for the fancy high rises in NY, you know? Mortgaged themselves to the hilt. To this day, I swear on the utilities. They're like the OG subscription services. I mean, it was so obvious. It's really hard knowing you're so much smarter than your parents. You know?"

Logan pressed himself up. "Okay Sascha, I'll have the pilot turn around and we will drop you off. You have a date that you need to show up for." Sascha Toner was one of the most important figures in the tech world. He wasn't about to risk his life by taking him on a wild goose chase around the Congo.

"Oh, the pilot will go wherever I tell him," Sascha said. "And the model? I set her and her girlfriends up with a luxurious night in San Francisco and I apologized and used a work excuse. So, she's not mad. She gets it. See? Everyone wins."

"Sascha, I promised your board that I would keep you

safe," Logan said. "Taking you into the DRC is going back on that promise. I need to get you home." He stared at Sascha in disbelief. "Okay, we are way past boundary crossing here. You're on the flight. It's a family emergency, and I am not working for you right now. Do you understand? I have to help my family. We will revisit this boundary issue later, because your dependency on me is very unhealthy."

"No, you're totally right," Sascha said, sitting in the aisle across from him. "What are you—"

"Shh!" Logan stared at his surveillance screen. Bringing Sascha Toner into the DRC would likely ruin his reputation in the security field. *No matter what, keep your subject in a safe environment at all times.* The DRC was not that. Not where he was going. "You can't... you can't come with me, Sascha. It's not safe. You can't buy my friendship." Logan regretted the last part. He took a sip from his flask to hide the discomfort.

"I didn't realize it was for sale," Sascha said.

"I'm sorry. I didn't mean that. Look, you may not realize it, but there's pressure in protecting you. From your handlers, from the government. They're all wondering where you are right now, I promise you. And I cannot protect you the way I need to where we're going."

A more sobered Sascha stood. "As entitled as I seem, sometimes I need to get away, too. Get out of reach of those people who surround me all day. They treat me with kid gloves. All the time. Like I'm the second coming, or something. Who knows? Maybe I'll keep you safe for once."

Logan laughed. "And how are you going to do that?"

"Tell me why we're going to the Congo, and I will make suggestions." The plane hit turbulence and Sascha quickly buckled himself in. He took deep breaths and closed his eyes. "I never get used to this."

The turbulence ended, and Sascha sighed. "So tell me,

why do you need to go to the DRC? Some secret spy shit? I've got great connections in Berlin. The Germans totally get me. And they still play their Nintendos, so..."

"Where we're going is not safe for you," Logan said. "That's why I would like to turn the plane around."

"We're well over the Pacific by now," Sascha said. He loosened his seatbelt and quickly tightened it again. "I'm going where you're going."

"No," Logan said. "The board would never approve it. So, may I please turn this plane around?"

Sascha chewed an ice cube. "My assistant... she'll set up base camp in Kinshasa. It's no biggie, really." Sascha hit the button, and the steward appeared. "Another, please. Maybe three ice cubes. My mouth needs something to do." He turned to Logan. "So tell me why."

Logan hated blurring the lines of professionalism, but he felt he had no choice. "You just needle and you dig, and you want to know about my life. It makes it really hard to work with you."

"Well, I'm sorry if I have come to appreciate you as a complete human being. Excuse me for caring. And now you have made me sound like my mother, so thank you."

Logan sighed. "My wife appears to be in some kind of trouble."

Sascha nearly jumped out of his seat. "Your wife? How did my background check miss that?"

"Because I know how to keep things private," Logan said. "And we're... estranged. For about a year now. We've just never officially split."

"You're a surprising man," Sascha said. "What I wouldn't give for a wife, and you have one on the other side of the world, languishing."

"Freya is definitely not languishing. She doesn't have it

in her bones." Logan laughed. "The woman acts before she thinks. About everything. I proposed us slowing down, maybe starting a family, but she... she will never stop moving. This?" He said, pointing to his laptop. "I'm pretty sure that this time she's pissed off the wrong people. At least, I'm guessing."

"What do you mean, you're guessing? You don't know what's going on?" Sascha sat beside Logan and grabbed his laptop. "Give me that."

"You probably won't find out anything my network doesn't already know."

Sascha typed quickly, as screens popped up right and left. "Oh, the army network? I would say about ninety percent of mid-level hackers can get into any military system they want to."

"Then why don't they?" Logan asked.

"They want their tax refunds."

Logan recalled Sascha's storied history as a tween hacker. Arrested by the FBI at twelve for hacking into Las Vegas casino security systems, he was given leniency on the condition that he keep his grades up and enlighten the government engineers on his uncanny abilities.

"So why is your wife... ex... in trouble?" Sascha asked.

"It seems she has acquired some new, high-powered enemies," Logan said.

"What makes you think so?"

"Her sister messaged me," Logan said. "Something cryptic. An old code word we used when one of us needed help."

"What's the code word?" Sascha asked.

"We're going to the county fair."

Sascha chuckled. "What are the county fairs like in the Congo?"

Logan nearly choked on his drink as he felt himself relaxing into conversation with Sascha.

"What?" Sascha laughed. "I imagine they're lively."

"Have you ever wanted to be a part of a different family? From the second I met Freya, I didn't ever want to be apart from her. And then, her sisters, despite their quirks… and Howard, always drinking, and their gorilla…"

"They have a gorilla?"

Logan shrugged. "Binta is our brother. Howard always said that he needed Binta and Chidi more than they needed him. And that was true. Needless to say, I wanted to be a part of this family from the second Freya brought me into the hot mess that it was or is. They're my family. They have been for a long time now, despite the distance."

"You're still in love with her," Sascha said.

Logan looked up. "Don't you dare tell her that." He straightened up. "I need to check out the scene and make sure they're okay."

"We're going to check out the scene," Sascha said.

"Sascha, I can't let you leave Kinshasa. I will hire guards who will escort you to a secured hotel immediately. If people know you're in the DRC, you will be an instant target."

"From the looks of it, no one is here," Sascha said, pulling up the jungle image on his laptop.

"I can't protect you in that space the way you need to be protected."

"I release you of all liability."

Logan turned to the screen and stared at the image of the jungle. "The jungle is different. There are a million ways to die, and it's as if they all seek you out. I need you to understand that."

Sascha kicked back his drink and bristled as it burned

his tongue. "I can handle a few snakes." He gazed blankly at the aisles ahead of them. "Maybe I will just stay at base camp. Maybe that's the best plan."

Logan chuckled. "Trust me. The secured hotel. If the board finds out..."

"Fuck the board," Sascha said. "I need an adventure." He turned to Logan's laptop and zoomed in on Chidi's lab. All looked quiet as the lights went out.

Logan closed his eyes, wishing he could just speak to Freya. He turned out his light and tried to sleep, but his temple throbbed with the growing certainty that Freya was in deep trouble.

16

The cool dawn light found Chidi's home bustling with activity. Joseph and Albert, Hugo's guards, collected on the front lawn as gaggles of parrots flew from tree to tree and introduced the morning with a cacophony of fluttering squawks. They would start off early before the balmy heat of mid-morning set in, followed by the incessant afternoon lethargy. Without knocking, Hugo entered Freya's room and found Chidi wrapping Freya's torso with a support band. A purple bruise poked out of the top of the band where she'd slammed into the desk the night before.

"Ready to go?" Hugo asked.

"I should ask you the same question," Freya said. "You have supplies?"

Hugo nodded. "We have what we need."

Chidi gave Freya a knowing look. These men would die, and fast.

"Just remember," Hugo said. "My Kinshasa connections

are on standby. I give them the word, and they will jump at the chance to kill either or both of your sisters. I've offered them a very generous bounty. If you want to see Jules or Chidi again, all you have to do is keep me alive."

"Oh, we're all going to die," Freya said. She buttoned her shirt and stood to face Hugo. "It's just a matter of when, and how long, we will suffer."

"Your negative outlook better not get us killed." Hugo stalked out.

Moments later, Freya heard him yelling directions at his men; something along the lines of acquiring more supplies. She gathered a rain slicker and her pack. Since she was being forced to attend her own death march, she would introduce Hugo to every delight the jungle had to offer.

Have you heard from our brother? Freya signed to Chidi.

Not yet, Chidi signed. Binta had made it off the property without issue, but she'd hoped he hadn't dared to venture back. The sisters often worried that they'd domesticated him too much. He never liked staying away for long.

You know that I can only get so far without him, Freya signed.

Chidi nodded. The Blue family operated from scientific standpoints, except for a few superstitions that had been instilled in them since birth. Howard loved to sit in a field and jot down notes on primate behavior, but he also loved pushing the storied histories of the Congolese tribes into the girls' heads. Night after night, they sat by the fire and listened to the histories of the kings and queens who had ruled the land. As much as they publicly scoffed at Isolde and the myth, something inside of them held a reverence for Isolde and her jungle; an odd gratitude and wish to be in her favor.

Binta's family history was closely tied to the volcano and

its inhabitants. Till the day he died, Howard told story after story of how Binta hailed from the same pack of gorillas that guarded the volcano. Jungle lore maintained that an immortal silverback led a devoted pack of offspring that was sworn to stop intruders from stealing the treasure; Isolde's chosen high guard. He was the stuff of nightmares, the story Congolese grandmothers told their grandkids to keep them out of the jungle. It was said that the vicious ape sired generations of gorillas bound to Isolde's curse. While his packs died out, he had remained young and virile for centuries, so the story went. If anyone made it near the volcano's entrance, they would never live to tell about it.

One late summer afternoon, when Howard was feeling especially bold after drinking two bottles of wine, he left his camp site and scaled the side of the volcano, nearly dying twice, by his own accounts. The first time, an apparition lifted him through the sharp bramble he'd tumbled into during his ascent. The second time, he was pulled up from the side of the volcano's ledge by a female gorilla with amber eyes. She beckoned him to follow her, leading to what he thought was her baby, before running off to join her pack.

As he neared the volcano's peak, he discovered an abandoned baby gorilla, near death and crying out for its pack. The sight of Binta sobered him. He scooped up the infant and escaped down the side of the mountain before the pack came sniffing around. He nursed Binta back to health and adopted him as family. Binta was adopted just before Chidi. The two bounced around the Blue back yard together as babies, blissfully unaware of their differences. Binta was the reason Freya became enamored with primates.

If Freya was able to make it up to the volcano, she would need Binta's help facing off with the pack that guarded its entrance. If her father's story was true, Binta had the silverback's blood. Howard suspected that he was rejected because he wasn't overpowered by Isolde's curse the way the others were. The pack recognized his difference and rejected him.

"Too sweet for that pack," Howard was frequently heard saying, as Binta rolled in the grass with Chidi. The gorilla had a heightened sensitivity and intelligence seldom seen in his species. He quickly learned to sign, adopted empathy, and was especially careful not to play rough with little Chidi, who saw him as her equal. Binta would lead Howard to interesting discoveries in the jungle, enriching his research. Jules and Freya called Binta, Howard, and Chidi, the three musketeers.

The local Nganga was a spiritualist healer who noted Binta's unique strength. When Howard and the family passed by, the man would bow at Binta's presence. Young Binta, often shy when first meeting strangers, meandered up to the man and placed his hand on his bowed head. The man slowly looked up and smiled, a tear streaming down his face. "Saveur," the man uttered, a toothless grin appearing across his face.

"Why does that man call Binta a savior?" Chidi asked.

"He thinks Binta is the one to save us all, I suppose," Howard said.

Freya rolled her eyes at the time, but as the years passed, she'd come to see Binta's powers. He had not only saved her from numerous life-or-death situations, but he had a deep connection to the jungle. It welcomed Binta. Other animals flocked to him, flowers bloomed in his path, the jungle nurtured him and was his mother in place of the one that abandoned him.

Binta will be there, Chidi signed. *He will protect you.*

If we make it that far, Freya signed.

17

~

The sky was clear and the sunrise a caramel orange, as they made their way through the choppy, seldom-tread back trail. Freya quickly noted that Hugo's ragtag group of British and Congolese guards—seven in total—were unaccustomed to jungle treks. They muttered misgivings to each other when out of Hugo's earshot, regretting joining his lot in the first place. She imagined that he must've cobbled them together through the Kinshasa black market, an underground network of thieves and pirates no upstanding diamond businessman ever wanted to admit mingling with, but oftentimes their only connection to the miners in more remote areas.

Albert kept his rifle pointed at her back. Though she felt Hugo's violent, unstable gaze burning through her as she led the group, she could do nothing but continue walking and plot their next steps through the thick brush. Every now and then she would stop and glance skyward, peering at the volcano's peak through her binoculars. Head down and determined to plod forward, Hugo would huff as he ran into the guard directly in front of him.

The further that they ascended, the more triggered Hugo became. Her father's foreboding tone echoed in her mind. *Walk into the jungle with a foolish man at your side, you likely won't walk out.* Freya was certain that Hugo's impetuousness would lead to everyone's death. It didn't matter how many men he had guarding him; he didn't honor the jungle. He only wanted to steal from it. One misstep could send the guards behind him down the side of a mountain. They could brush up against poisonous flora; any number of dangers Freya hoped they could avoid. As much as she loathed the sight of him, any threat to his life meant death for Jules and Chidi. She had to keep this fool alive.

The dense air of the lowlands hit her as they approached the entrance to the back trail. She found herself out of shape and panting. Those behind her were much worse off. From the sound of his gasps, one of Hugo's guards had severe asthma. He wouldn't survive the altitude. They traipsed over choppy ground that gave way to thick mud and high grasses. She tied her rain slicker around her waist and stepped carefully. It was easy to get stuck in the marsh.

"Step carefully," Freya said. The second the words left her mouth, Albert fell face forward into the mud and a stray bullet flew past Hugo, grazing the side of Joseph's leg. He cried out as Freya and the rest of the group ducked in fear of getting hit.

"Jesus, man!" Hugo said. "What is wrong with you?"

Albert dropped his rifle and tried to push himself out of the marsh, but he was stuck. He looked up at Hugo with pleading eyes, as his legs sank into the fresh quicksand. Hugo nodded to two guards close by who stepped carefully around him and, with great effort, pulled him out. No one wanted to say what Freya was thinking. *The curse.* The group silently resumed their trek.

They made it to the lowlands by nightfall the next day. The fenced entrance to the back trail was littered with warning signs written in French. *Take the back trail and die. The curse begins now. Welcome to Isolde's jungle.* Albert muttered to himself in French as he took in the ominous messages. A British guard chuckled and shook his head. Joseph and the others said nothing, but gazed past the signs to the jungle beyond, their faces ashen. Hugo stepped ahead of Freya and pulled on the old lock. He signaled to one of his men, who came forward with bolt cutters and removed it. Hugo pushed the creaking gate open.

He turned to Freya, a wicked smile across his lips. "Ladies first."

Freya hesitantly stepped past him and located the overgrown path entrance. A deep lethargy overcame her as her foot hit the ground and her dubious belief in the curse gave way to acute fear. *I mean no harm, Isolde. Please, please protect me.* Her pleas would likely do no good. It was said that Isolde was a fierce, protective mother who wielded the powers of the jungle to her purpose. Not only was she hoarding the jewels, she held tight to her beloved child's hand. All Freya could do was beg for mercy and protection.

As the rest of Hugo's men crossed the gated threshold, Freya felt the jungle come alive. Normally at this hour, its inhabitants would settle into a quiet patter like the rest of the world. Only the nocturnal creatures of the jungle would stay awake and stand guard. But with the arrival of these visitors, the jungle had awakened. Freya suspected that the curse was in motion, though the scientist in her wanted to believe that there was no evidence to support such a thing;

only years of watching treasure hunters disappear into the jungle to never return.

"Why are we taking this route? It appears no one else has for years," Hugo said.

Freya faced him. "I want my sisters safe as much as you want your treasure. This route shaves two days off our journey."

"But it's more perilous, yes? Are you trying to get us killed?"

"If you prefer to take the park route, that's not a problem. I'll have you there in five days."

Hugo sighed, his head tilted from side to side, pondering the decision. "We'll take this route."

"Good," Freya said. "Expect long, difficult days. And I would remove that vest."

Hugo bristled. "And get myself killed? Yeah, right."

"Suit yourself," Freya said. "That will weigh you down and cause you to dehydrate faster. And if you come face to face with any jungle inhabitants, a vest won't stop them from gutting you."

Freya continued on the path, stepping slowly through the last part of the marsh. The men mimicked her steps, not wanting to face their fate before even reaching the base of the mountain. The grasses became higher. Freya paused before spotting the hidden trail. Hugo's guards hacked away at the overgrown grass with machetes. The ground grew firmer, and they gained elevation. The air thinned, and all she could hear were the men behind her, panting for air as their lungs adjusted to the altitude.

Freya inspected the ground, making sure she was following the old trailhead correctly. Mostly overgrown by grass, she could make out age-old marks in the dirt, likely from foot traffic. The trail had existed before the park was designated protected territory. The tribes that roamed the land were hunters just as much as the animals that inhabited it. They were probably just going about their day, foraging for food. Nevertheless, before the back trail was locked in the sixties, treasure hunters with a greed like Hugo's attempted to scale it.

Park officials banned the back trail after too many bodies started showing up near the base. The bodies hadn't been ravaged by jungle predators, as one might expect. Rather, they were found in unimaginable situations, oddly preserved like mummies, hanging from impossibly high tree limbs. They died unnatural deaths. Isolde and her curse were always credited, of course. Locals made effigies and prayed to Isolde to have mercy on them, to protect their farms, make them bountiful. During the rainy season, Freya could often see Isolde's likeness painted on tree trunks, sometimes carved into the dirt. The rains inevitably washed them away, but her presence and power over the jungle lingered.

Freya pushed the tall grass away as she continued toward the base of the mountain. She glanced up at the peak. Though it was dormant, she'd become used to the constant cloud of steam and gases that rose from it. The base was covered for a mile around in white clouds that hid the canopy of rich flora that grew from the volcanic rock; an untouched habitat protected from the rest of the park's stream of visitors. From there, it would be a hike through the thick jungle that she hadn't dared visit since she was much younger. The final part of the climb, if they made it, would be up the side of the volcano itself, through porous, steaming rock and sulfur clouds.

They were far enough away from civilization that they would never find their way back without her. *The perfect opportunity to run*, she thought. No one would catch her. Hugo and his men probably wouldn't even know how to get out. But then the thought of Jules and Chidi in trouble erased the idea from her mind. *Get to the top as fast as you can. If you can.*

The grasses began obstructing Freya's view of the trail and the direction they were going. She pulled out her compass, tapped it, and peered up at the peak of the mountain. The compass needle was spinning in circles. *Is that you, old girl?* Freya thought. *Give me a break. At the very least, protect Jules and Chidi for me.*

Hugo leaned in beside her. "You don't know where we're going? I've got some religious fanatics back here who are having doubts. Let's get a move on before they change their mind."

"Anyone who tries to leave now will die," Freya said. "They'll get turned around in the grasses and wander for days until they die from dehydration or drink marsh water and die instead of bacterial infections. I know where we're going. We're almost to the lowlands. But I need your men to clear the path until we get there."

Hugo whistled and flagged over Joseph and Albert, who glanced at Freya with fearful looks.

"Les herbes deviennent plus hautes," one of the guards from the back called out. "Isolde est la." He'd noted the extraordinary height of the grass and that Isolde was the cause.

Freya shrugged, mentioning how tall the farmers' crops had grown that season, too. "Peut-etre. Et peut-être qu'elle est la raison pour laquelle vos récoltes ont grandi cette année." She directed them in French to chop down the grasses ahead of her and pointed to the volcano's peak, indicating that they should chop in that direction.

"What is this about crops?" Hugo asked in a near whisper to Freya.

"Isolde is the goddess of the jungle. She brings pain and sickness. She also brings the rains, which the farmers rely on to grow their crops. Most of the men here are farmers, I suspect. They pray to Isolde for abundance as much as they fear her wrath."

The guards mumbled in French to each other while clearing a path.

"What are they going on about now?" The British guard asked.

Freya glanced at the volcano's peak. "It is said that Isolde's tomb is guarded by a pack of cursed gorillas."

The British guard exchanged a smile with Hugo and started laughing.

Hugo looked at the sky and in jest said, "Dear Isolde, please call off your monkeys and stop hoarding the treasure." He grinned and broke into a sardonic laugh.

What did your father do to you? Freya thought. It was best to keep her thoughts to herself. Anything could unhinge Hugo. She imagined the jungle would tap into his madness at any time, and she would be his first target.

18

Chidi sat in the living room and tried to close her eyes. The two guards at either end seemed as bored as she was. She wasn't used to sitting still for very long. She pressed herself up.

"I can't sleep here," Chidi said. "I need to go to my bedroom. And... I need to use the bathroom."

The guards looked at each other before one shrugged his approval.

"Thank you," Chidi said. She closed the bathroom door after one of the guards inspected it. Her first instincts were to climb out of the bathroom window, but it proved too small, and who knew what might happen to Jules and Freya if she actually escaped. At least she had a moment of privacy. She splashed water on her face, rubbed her eyes, and sat in the bathtub, momentarily closing her eyes to the nightmare she'd found herself in. She wished she could burrow into Binta's chest, a common comfort since she was a small child. The massive gorilla was a big, fluffy pillow in a little girl's eyes. *Who knows? Maybe I won't make it to see him again.*

She heard a knock at the door and instinctually crouched inside the bathtub. She didn't want to be the target of any stray bullets, should these guards meet someone they didn't like. Maybe Grace had seen her odd message and flagged it for the local authorities. Chidi heard a conversation outside, followed by yelling. The door to the bathroom suddenly flew open against the weight of one of the guards. He pointed his gun at her and directed her out to the living room, where the other guard had his weapon trained on a man she'd never seen before.

"Il dit qu'il vend des bibles," the guard said.

"Selling bibles?" Chidi asked, incredulously.

A white man she'd never seen before, in the middle of the jungle, selling bibles. It had to be a joke. "Je ne connais pas cet homme," Chidi responded, noting that she didn't know him.

"What are you saying?" the man asked. "I skipped French class, of course. Now I'm kicking myself."

"Ne lui pas dessus. Il attirera l'attention," Chidi begged the guard not to shoot him. It would bring unneeded attention.

"Il est américain," the guard shouted at Chidi. "L'ami de Freya." She questioned whether she should say the stranger was Freya's friend. In hindsight, it could put him in more danger.

The guard shoved the man on the couch and pointed his rifle directly at him. He cowered under the threat of the weapon. He looked past the guard at something running toward them. The sound was sudden, but unmistakable. The guard turned to face the oncoming threat, but it was too late.

Binta toppled the guard and pinned him to the ground as the stranger jumped behind the couch. The second guard pointed his rifle at Chidi and pulled her toward him. Binta's gaze focused on the other guard. He rose up when the man fired a shot into the ceiling. Binta backed away at the sound.

"Laisse moi lui parler," Chidi whispered, begging the guard to allow her to get Binta to back down.

His hand shaking, the guard pointed his gun at Binta. He pulled the safety, preparing to shoot.

Another figure entered the scene, causing Chidi and the stranger to audibly exhale at the same time. Logan. After securing the weapon on the floor, he stepped in front of the man's shot. But Binta moved past him, growling.

"Posez votre arme!" The lone guard yelled.

"Put your weapon down," Logan said. "You've got a pissed off gorilla here. I'm your best friend right now. Make the right decision, before he tears you a new face."

The guard trained his weapon on Binta. "Je meurs, il meurt."

"Bad choice," Logan said. In mere seconds, Logan aimed, took a shot, and the guard fell to the floor.

Chidi broke down crying, and Binta padded over to her, every bit the innocent brother she loved. She embraced him and sobbed into his coat, which was matted with dried blood. "I thought you wouldn't come."

"I think the trauma of what I just experienced will never leave my body." The stranger rose, keeping his eyes on the remaining guard Logan had pinned down.

"I told you to stay put in the jeep," Logan said as he tied the guard's hands.

Chidi ran to Logan and embraced him as the guard struggled under Logan's weight. "I knew you'd come." She glanced at the stranger and whispered. "Who is this?"

Logan wiped his brow. "This is one of my clients who unexpectedly tagged along. Sascha, this is Chidinma Blue, my..."

Chidi smiled. "I'm still your sister. We're still your family."

Logan scratched the back of his head and awkwardly changed the subject. "I need to check the grounds and secure this one in the shed. Don't let Sascha out of your sight. He likes to wander."

Binta turned his sights on Sascha and approached. Sascha wilted into the couch, avoiding eye contact as Binta proceeded to sniff him from head to toe.

"What do I do?" Sascha whispered. "I look away, right? Or is that black bears?"

"Binta means no harm," Chidi said.

"Excuse me, but I heard rumors that he likes to rip faces off," Sascha said. "So if it's okay with you, I would like tips on how to remain on his good side."

"Stay still and let him get used to you," Chidi said, smiling. "That's all."

Binta sat on his haunches with his hand resting on Sascha's. His softened gaze watched Sascha's every movement.

Chidi smiled, wiping her face. "Oh, I get it. You remind Binta of Papa. It happens with white men sometimes."

"Papa?" Sascha asked in a whisper. "Hopefully fond memories?"

"Yes, very," Chidi said. "Binta's my brother. We were raised together."

"Oh," Sascha said, still quivering under the gorilla's presence. "And you're handling this capture and guns thing really well, I might add. Just an everyday thing. No biggie."

"Welcome to the Congo," Chidi said. "And take Logan

seriously, if you want to stay alive. You are not in California anymore." Chidi took one big exhale, before stalking over to the kitchen, while Sascha remained immobile under the gorilla's newfound friendship.

Binta sneezed and held his gaze on Sascha. He tightened his grip on Sascha's hand.

"That's okay," Sascha said. "We can sit here as long as you want. I'm a good conversationalist. Especially when I'm nervous. I should state from the outset that I would like to live."

"Do you like tea?" Chidi called over. "It might make us all feel better for a moment." She was good at that. Finding the small comforts during disastrous times.

"I can get you anything you could ever want," Sascha continued. "Bananas for days. I especially like my nose, so please stay away from that. But you don't care about money, do you? That's refreshing. You just want to hold my hand."

Binta sneezed again, and Sascha slowly lifted his hand to wipe off his face.

"Allergic to Jewish people? I hope not. I plan to be your very best friend. Have you been to Palo Alto? I think my engineers would love you. You could... keep the workflow going."

Sascha went silent as Binta stared him down. The gorilla climbed onto the couch, dragging the tech CEO along. He pulled Sascha's head into his chest.

"Okay, this is happening," Sascha said. "I'm fine with it, as long as you are. Just don't expect me to call you the very next day, you know?"

Binta grunted, which caused Sascha to shut up.

Logan entered, took one look at Sascha, and shook his head. "I think I need to hire Binta. He's the only being on the planet that can shut you up."

"Very... funny." Sascha stared ahead, his cheek pressed against Binta's chest. "So, can you help me out here?"

Chidi walked over with tea, and she and Logan collapsed in the chairs opposite Binta and Sascha. Chidi offered Sascha tea, but he waved it away.

"Binta," Chidi signed. "He needs space."

"No, no," Logan said, bemused. "He turned down a date with a supermodel to hijack my trip," Logan said.

"It was during working hours," Sascha said, as Binta placed a hand over Sascha's other cheek. "You never informed me you were leaving."

"This is what you get," Logan responded. He sipped his tea, satisfied with the scene.

"I can handle constructive criticism," Sascha said.

"No, you can't. You cannot handle constructive criticism. If you could, you would be on a date right now with a beautiful Latvian woman."

"She was Estonian."

"Instead, you're being embraced by a male primate who has apparently adopted you as his child." Logan rubbed his eyes.

There was momentary silence as the three contemplated that they were drinking tea while Jules and Freya were god knows where.

"You know what?" Sascha asked, his voice muffled. "I am appreciating that there's no small talk here. But, back to things. What the fuck is happening here?"

Logan turned to Chidi before eyeing the guard. "Chidi, he's right. What's Freya done now?"

~

19

They made it to the base of the mountain around ten PM. Freya signaled for everyone to stop and take a break. They had at least a few more hours of hiking before they would set up camp and rest for the night. Hugo approached Freya, clearly strung out from lack of sleep and whatever drugs he was on.

"Why are we stopping?" he asked.

"Everyone is exhausted," Freya said. "We need rest before we continue."

Hugo leaned in. "Remember what's at stake."

"Oh, I haven't forgotten. And I will need to check in with my sisters before we continue."

Hugo's hands balled into fists. He took a deep breath and focused on the ground. "I say when we check in with your sisters." He nodded to Albert, who approached her with restraints in hand.

Freya saw the restraints and felt her heart race. In a second, that need to physically defend herself came rushing back. Black Adder training was imprinted in Freya's bones, and in a knee-jerk reaction, she disarmed Albert and had him on the ground. "I don't care if I live or die, but I will not be restrained." She turned and glanced at Hugo before releasing Albert. "And if you go back on your word, I will make your death slow and painful."

Hugo smiled. "I can tell you were the more challenging daughter. Capturing Jules was so easy. And Chidi—well, she's just along for the ride. But what is it with you—"

"I speak to my sisters, or I don't continue on," Freya said. "Without me, you and all of your men will die within five minutes."

Hugo wiped his brow and nodded, before walking away to relieve himself. "Get them online," Hugo said. "The sooner we do, the sooner this one shuts up."

"Ou est ma soeur?" Freya whispered to Albert, asking him where Jules was.

Albert looked around to make sure Hugo wasn't within earshot. "S'il intend, nous mourns thus les deus."

She could appeal to the Congolese guards. They were in it because they didn't have a choice, she assumed. "Dis-moi, et je t'aiderai, a retriever ta famille." Her appeal worked. Family was everything to the Congolese.

"Quartier Mont Amba," Albert continued. "Un entrepôt."

A warehouse in Kinshasa. She could hint to Chidi when she spoke with her.

"Merci."

"Je veux aller a la maison." He wanted to go home, like the rest of them. He quietly informed her that Hugo wiped out his and the other guards' family debts and freed them from service if they got him to the top of the mountain. Miners like Hugo virtually enslaved generations of

Congolese families by way of buying their families' homes, or helping with medical treatments. If they didn't go, their families would be killed.

Albert quickly turned away as Hugo approached her with the iPad. She could barely make out the outline of Jules, though the screen cut in and out. Freya grabbed the small device.

"Jules, it's Freya. Are you okay?"

Jules sat in a light-filled room. She slowly nodded, not uttering a word.

"Have they hurt you?"

"As long as I keep my mouth shut, I'm okay," Jules responded. "Which is terribly hard for me, as you know." She slurred her words. "Don't make your choices based on whether I live or die. Get yourself out of there. Please."

At this, the internet access cut out, and the screen froze.

"Jules?" Freya said. "Jules!" She looked at Hugo and his guard. "I need to get her back."

"Must be the load shedding. Nothing I can do. Try calling the other one," he instructed the guard.

The guard dialed a number, and the device started ringing again. After a minute, a guard answered.

"Put her on," Hugo said.

Chidi's familiar voice chimed in. "I thought you might be dead."

"No, sis," Freya said. "We're at the base. Are they treating you okay?"

"Jesus," Chidi said. "Don't forget your rope. You know?"

Freya nodded. Rainy season. "I have it."

Hugo grabbed the device and cut off the call. "Okay, enough family reunions for one day. Now, we go." He grabbed the device from Freya and nearly jumped at the oncoming guard, who ran up and whispered in his ear.

"Park rangers," Hugo said, turning to Freya. "You took us on a route with park rangers?" He looked at his guards. "Hide your weapons. We are on a nice hike, just like the rest of the people who vacation here."

A nice hike on a never-used trail in the middle of the night. Makes total sense, Freya thought.

After a couple minutes, two rangers approached. Freya recognized one as Beno. He took stock of the large group and saw Freya. He walked up to her and Hugo.

"Good evening," Beno said. He nodded at Freya, his eyes searching her for some reason they were on the back trail. "Dr. Blue. Awfully late for a hike, isn't it?"

Beno's co-ranger was checking the scene as Hugo's guards surrounded them. Freya's goal was to get them out of there safely. Nothing—especially these rangers—was going to stop Hugo. She concocted a story that she hoped would save their lives. A smile crossed Freya's face as she tried to play off the awkward situation. "My friend is only visiting for a short while, and he wanted to do something different... special. And you know me. I'm always up for a challenge."

Beno nodded, looking around at the scene. It was clear Freya was in trouble. She could sense he was thinking of ways to get her out of this mess.

"You know, the gate on the main trail is locked until the morning, and we didn't want to waste time," Freya said. "I promise you, Ben—I will keep them safe. Can you give me a pass this once? You know—just like my teenage days, eh?"

"Only Howard isn't here to rescue you," Beno said, looking her squarely in the eye. "Though I feel him most days in this jungle... talking to the animals like he always did."

"I know this back trail better than anyone," Freya said.

"Howard taught me well. I promise. Nothing exciting will happen."

"Let me introduce myself," Hugo said, cutting the awkward tension. "Jean, Freya's friend."

Beno shook Hugo's hand, not without hesitation. "Dr. Blue has taken you up quite a precarious route. And it's against park rules to be here. The back trail is forbidden. I'm afraid you'll have to turn around."

As Hugo signaled his guard to take action, Freya said, "Beno, you know me. I wouldn't do anything to harm anyone. Please." She looked at him pleadingly and squeezed his hand. "Let me show them notre belle montagne. Please. Plus, you don't want to be escorting all us smelly hikers down the mountain when the rains set in, do you?" Freya smiled. "Let me show them a little bit more, and I promise we will head back down."

A new awareness crossed Beno's face. *She was in trouble, yes. But he would be in trouble if he didn't leave immediately.*

Beno squeezed Freya's hand back and nodded. A sense of urgency commingled with concern as he quickly moved to exit the scene. He turned to Hugo. "Well, you're in good hands. Dr. Blue knows this mountain better than anyone. Radio us, if you need anything at all." Beno's eyes locked with Freya's as he turned quickly to go.

Hugo waved and said, "Nice to meet you," as they moved through the grasses. Hugo's gaze followed them until they were gone.

"You're lucky," Hugo said to Freya, before turning away to speak to two of his guards.

Freya watched as he exchanged words with the two guards, who picked up their rifles and followed Beno's steps away from the base of the mountain. Hugo stalked past her and stopped when he saw she was standing still, her gaze following Beno's footsteps.

"It's time to go," Hugo said.

Freya didn't hear anything but the sounds of the jungle as they approached the canopy overhead. It wasn't until about an hour later that she noticed the two guards had returned. She put one foot in front of the other, numb from the thought that Beno and the other ranger were likely dead. *My fault*, she thought. *They might be dead because of me.* She trained her gaze on Hugo. *Isolde, save him, please. And protect my sisters. I need your strength.*

At the plea, Freya felt a light pattering of raindrops hit her face. As the rains intensified, her feet slipped on the muddy path they were clearing. Isolde would do her bidding. The queen always enjoyed a good death.

20

They hiked early into the morning and finally made it to the base, just as the rains started again. Hugo and his men struggled to clear the old trail as the thick white clouds surrounded them and blocked their view. Freya heard Hugo lose his footing in the mud behind her and hoped that he would be swept away. Though she'd hiked this far, the constant appeal of making a run for it plagued her with each step. But as the thick humid air surrounded her, she realized she couldn't turn around now. She glanced down at her compass and realized it was pointing the wrong direction. *Am I going mad?* She knew they were on the right path.

Just ahead Freya saw a clearing that might be suitable for a stop. Everyone was exhausted, and she needed the clouds to lift so they could see the path forward. She could see the canopy of ancient, volcanic trees that loomed above the small opening. Freya hoped they would provide enough cover from the rains that they would be able to get sleep.

Some of the men collapsed against tree trunks into an instant slumber, the raindrops hitting their faces.

"Take precautions with the rain," Freya said.

The men who hadn't already passed out located the nearest trees and secured themselves to them with ropes and belts.

Hugo approached her. "What does that mean? Precautions?"

"The rain turns the ground to mud. If it continues with this intensity, there will be mudslides." Freya spotted a path that might provide privacy for her to relieve herself.

"Where are you going?"

"I need privacy," Freya said.

Hugo followed her. "Don't worry, I will look away. I can't risk you leaving now."

Hugo followed her down the path. As they moved away from the guards, Freya realized that the western edge of the mountain base was mere steps away from where she would relieve herself. She could easily nudge Hugo over the edge and likely make it back in one piece. The need to act rose within her. How could she trust that he or any number of his men wouldn't kill she and her sisters the second he made it to the diamond? Freya asked herself this question over and over.

Freya pushed down her pants as Hugo turned away. She could hear a massive waterfall below them, just over the mountainside. Her Adder training heightened her sense of opportunity. *The jungle offers you every opportunity to get the upper hand,* her Adder commander would say. *Use it to your advantage.* She could tell his men that he fell, and she would pay them instead for their troubles.

"Hurry up, would you?" Hugo demanded.

She silently stood and pulled up her pants. Hugo was

gazing at a printed drawing of the diamond of Isolde. She recognized it from the old books Howard used to pour through. It caught her off guard. Just before she was about to grab Hugo from behind and toss him over the edge of the mountain, she stopped. The image of the diamond paralyzed her, and she found herself so close to Hugo's shoulder that she could smell his skin. He whipped around, unsettled at her proximity.

"Isolde's diamond," Freya said. "Why are men obsessed with it?"

Hugo stepped away from Freya and put the picture in his pocket. "My father loved the diamond more than he loved his own family. I will have the one thing he never could."

"Why would you want something so cursed?"

"Why does anyone want anything? Because you spend a lifetime pondering something. It's the purest diamond in existence. And I'm going to have it."

"Are you going to stare at it for the rest of your life? Look what happened to Isolde."

"I'm going to enjoy the memory of taking it from her. It will be priceless." Hugo said.

Freya was stunned at his hubris. Locals never dared to speak against Isolde. She looked up at the black clouds overhead and felt the rains intensify. "The diamond belongs to her. If you even were able to find it, it would bring you a lifetime of misery."

"I will find it," Hugo said. "And misery? I've experienced that already. So, let your queen bring her worst."

Lightning flashed overhead, followed closely by a lingering roll of thunder.

"My father searched his whole life for the diamond, and the bastard never got it," Hugo continued. "I'm going to get the one thing he never could." Hugo glanced at the sky as the rains pelted his face and laughed. "I'm coming for you!"

Hugo pushed Freya back up the mountainside to the clearing where his guards were sleeping. The Congolese guards were high in the trees, strapped in, while the two British guards lay sprawled on the ground, despite the discomfort.

Freya strapped a rope to her side and started climbing a tree. "You might want to tell them to start climbing." Freya reached for the first limb and tested her weight against it. She continued climbing and finally settled in under the cover of two adjoining, leafy limbs that intertwined with an opposing tree's limbs, adding extra support. She secured herself to the tree with the rope and covered herself with her rain slicker and blanket. "Get to higher ground and hold on."

Hugo kicked the two guards on the ground. "I'm paying you to watch her."

Hugo jumped to the first limb of an opposing tree and climbed to a branch opposite Freya's, before strapping himself in. "Sweet dreams. I've decided that I don't believe your lore. It's monsoon season, that's all. We're going to find the bones of a dead queen and rip the diamond from her hands." Hugo closed his eyes, satisfied with his justification for the intense weather.

Freya closed her eyes and thought of her sisters. They had experienced the heavy rains as children. Howard took them on camping expeditions throughout the jungle while he conducted research. While they were never at this altitude, she recalled being covered from head to toe in mud, as they played in mud slides, as though they were at a theme park.

21

~

Hints of orange cloaked the skyline as dawn set in, and the grounds of Chidi's home came alive with activity. Exotic birds squawked overhead, as the occasional howler monkey disrupted the calm serenity of the trees surrounding her house. Chidi felt a presence behind her, tracing her steps as she crossed the lawn to the lab. She turned and Sascha stopped in his tracks, holding up his hands.

"Sorry," he said. "So sorry. I couldn't sleep. I didn't mean to frighten you."

She turned away and continued walking. "It's fine." Her mind was so distracted; all she could think about was her sisters. "Come on."

Sacha caught up to her. She could see from the way he wrung his hands that he was agitated. "It's just that, twenty-four hours ago, Logan was helping me pick out a suit, and now I've seen him murder a man, and I can't... I can't get it out of my head."

"Being forced to take a life makes you appreciate freedom that much more," Chidi said, watching her feet step through the grass. "Logan is a man of morals. But if he is pushed, he will defend himself. It's my understanding that he wanted to protect you from all of this. That you weren't supposed to tag along. Hmm?"

Sascha blushed. "You say that as though he's been keeping some dark secret from his beloved child."

Chidi unlocked the door to her lab, before turning to him. "He hasn't told me who you are. And I don't ask because I know Logan." She walked in and left it ajar. "And it might be helpful for you to know that Logan likes to compartmentalize the different parts of his life. I'm his family. You're his client. The fact that we've even met is uncanny. He likes to keep things separate. Does that help you understand why he wasn't comfortable with you being here?" She flipped on the lights and walked in, toward her computer station.

Sascha followed closely behind. "Look, is it okay if I... hang with you for a bit? I know I don't know you, and... and you don't owe me anything, certainly. It's just that... I'm out of my element here. In case you hadn't noticed." He jumped when a female chimpanzee with three babies clinging to her sauntered past him into the lab.

Chidi crouched to meet them and grabbed a bowl of figs from her desk to give to them. Two of the babies climbed into her arms. She lifted one up to show Sascha. "These are my assistants. This... is Sascha."

The mother and her remaining baby walked over to a large area covered in soft mats and grass. She settled in and watched as Chidi cradled her babies. One gazed at Sascha with its deep brown eyes.

Sascha bit his nail and took in the scene. Chidi could tell

he was so stunned and exhausted from the day's events that he didn't know how to react.

"Here." She passed the male baby to Sascha, along with a plush chimpanzee toy, before using a crimson sash to wrap the other baby to her chest.

The baby clutched the toy and settled into Sascha's chest for a nap. "I… I can't move," Sascha said. "I don't want to ruin this, but like, should I be afraid? What shouldn't I do?"

"Just shut up and enjoy it," Chidi said.

Sascha looked aghast, but too wilted to protest.

"Follow me." Chidi guided him to an old, torn up couch that had seen too many days of cuddling chimpanzees. "Sit here and close your eyes. Chimpanzees have magical ways of relaxing you. When they're not tearing up your furniture."

Sascha sat and watched Chidi work from a distance. "I'll probably just stay here and whisper to you," he said to the baby chimpanzee. "You know, not all of us can just hit the pillow and fall asleep like this little guy here. Some of us haven't slept well since, you know, 1990."

"You have a busy mind," Chidi whispered. "That can be a good thing. You get things done."

"Most people call it madness."

"Well then, maybe you needed to come here to quiet your mind," Chidi said.

"Or witness a murder or two. Holy!" Sascha's jaw dropped as a family of elephants approached the door. Chidi walked over to greet them and gave them a bin of carrots and apples. The baby followed her through the wide lab door.

Before long, Sascha lay down on the couch and closed his eyes. Without the distraction, Chidi went through the motions checking various screens, as the baby chimpanzee napped against her chest. The baby elephant followed where it could and waited patiently for Chidi's return when it couldn't fit through this or that corridor. Normally, the repetitive nature of checking the day's stats calmed her. She liked the ritual of being with the animal visitors and analyzing data. But even the distraction of work couldn't help her escape the worry of what might be happening to her sisters.

After a while, she turned off the screens and dimmed the lights. When she closed her eyes, tears stained her cheeks. The thought of living in a world without her sisters felt foreign and cold. She envisioned it, and the thought made her temple throb. Eventually, she collapsed on the other end of the couch and fell asleep to the sound of the chimpanzees' light snoring.

When she woke, she saw Binta sitting near the mother chimpanzee. The other baby still snoozed on Sascha's chest. Chidi moved next to Binta on the mat and signed to him. She attached a small device to his arm and secured it with a band.

"You're sending him to find Freya," Sascha said, frozen under the sleeping baby chimpanzee.

"He's the only one who can make the trek. And he knows her scent. He'll locate her faster than any of us."

Binta munched on bamboo shoots, contented in Chidi's presence.

"It's a risk for you," Sascha said.

She turned to Sascha with tears in her eyes. "It's like I'm being forced to choose. He's my brother. I can't lose him too." She gazed at Binta and kissed him. "Logan says he might be able to track where they're keeping Jules. But I don't have the same hope of finding Freya. I can only hope that her dumb luck follows her this time as well. She's like a stupid cat, that one."

"Freya is a smart woman," Sascha said. "And she has you. I'm sure that's reason enough to stay alive."

Logan walked in. "Just got a message. A ranger showed up an hour ago. He was left for dead after running into Hugo."

Chidi covered her mouth and took a deep breath. "She's still alive."

She stood up and guided Binta outside as Logan and Sascha trailed behind. She knelt in front of Binta and signed to him after tucking a small handwritten note behind the device on his arm. *Find Freya. She's with bad men. Stay hidden from them.*

Binta responded. *Find Freya. Binta loves Chidi.* The gorilla pulled Chidi into an embrace. She nuzzled him as tears streamed down her cheek. Suddenly he was off, and she could only see the distant tree branches part as he bounded into the jungle.

She held her face and wiped away tears before stalking past Sascha and Logan with her head down. She shut the door to her lab and crawled next to the mother chimpanzee; watching the babies' chests rise and fall. She closed her eyes at the thought of losing her entire family in one short day.

~

22

Despite the constant rains, Freya managed to sleep for a short while. Every now and then she would open her eyes to find Hugo's gaze trained on her, but her exhaustion forced her back to sleep. It wasn't until she heard the cries from Hugo's men that she jerked awake. Still secured to her tree, she looked down to find that the path they'd forged gave way to the deluge of rain. The muddy stream was a river below them, and the jungle floor was obscured. The water levels rose, as the rush of water pressed against the dense jungle shrubbery.

While most of Hugo's guards clung to their trees, one hadn't secured himself properly. He grasped to whatever branch he could reach but the water was stronger than his grip and he succumbed, his body washing away with the current. Two other guards grasped their ropes and took in air, struggling to climb higher before the water level submerged them. Bushes gave way to the pressure of the water, and Freya saw in the early dawn that the riverbank was eroding.

"We have to get to higher ground!" Freya shouted.

She unstrapped herself and tossed the rope around an opposing tree limb, before swinging across to another tree. She continued ascending, using the rope to climb even higher into the canopy, and lifting her legs away from the rising water level. Just as she secured herself, the roots of the tree she leapt from gave way and toppled into the rushing water. She continued her ascent, carefully securing herself to the next tree.

Hugo and his six remaining guards followed her lead, but with much less skill. He grasped younger limbs that broke off, before clambering up to the next. His men followed Freya as she moved between the trees, swinging on her rope from limb to limb. She turned back to see Hugo ascending with most of his men behind him. The riverbank they were just on was washed away in huge chunks, getting closer and closer to Hugo and his men. As the last of Hugo's guards made it over the edge of the cliff, the trees and riverbank disappeared behind him.

Hugo's guards were chattering in French and pointing at the volcano. *Too late to turn back now*, one of them said. *If we don't go, he will make our families suffer*, said another. *But Isolde will kill us anyway*, said a third. Freya was surprised it had taken this long for their fears to be acknowledged. *My father begged me not to go*, said another. *And now I will die on this mountain and bring shame to our family*. He started weeping.

"We keep moving," Hugo said, ascending to the next tree. "Come on!"

"I want to speak to my sisters before we continue," Freya said, the rain pelting her face.

"Make a call," Hugo said.

Albert shook his head. "It's gone. The rain... our connection is gone."

Freya turned away from them and fought against the hot tears that streamed down her face. She would no longer have a chance to talk to her sisters... to say goodbye. That was when she heard it. The deafening roar she'd only imagined from Howard's drunken tales.

"You're real," Freya whispered. It was the albino silverback. His growls echoed throughout the jungle in an ear-splitting shriek that made her cover her ears. A brisk wind followed, whipping the rain against their faces. In her mind, he'd been the stuff of Howard's stories; little more than a frightful tale, Howard told the girls around the campfire. Even so, she'd wanted it to be true.

She recalled Howard's tale of how the silverback towered over his pack, none of whom shared his albino coloring. *Isolde's chosen guard. He lives forever while his pack dies out and the next generation joins him.* Hugo and his guards shuddered as another deafening roar rang through the canopy. It was as if the albino knew she was coming all along. *Don't come here*, he warned. *Don't even try*. The rains continued, but the looming presence of the albino silverback retreated to the volcano's peak.

Some of Hugo's guards mumbled in French and made the sign of the cross. One inched down the tree and headed in the opposite direction, down the mountain.

"Where are you going?" Hugo said. Hugo glanced at Albert, who called out to the guard in French.

"He is going home," Albert said. "He is choosing which way he wants to die."

"He doesn't get to choose," Hugo said. "I get to choose."

Hugo nodded at his lone British guard, who whipped out a gun.

"Arret!" The British guard said.

The Congolese guard saw the gun pointed at him as he swung his rope to the tree below. He froze and raised his arms.

"He continues with us, or he dies now," Hugo said. "Along with his family." Hugo nodded to Albert, who translated for him.

The man tearfully nodded and made the sign of the cross as the British guard took aim.

"Stop," Freya said. "We need all the help we can get."

"What good is a guard who doesn't want to be here?" Hugo asked.

"None of us want to be here," Freya said.

Hugo closed his eyes, opened them, and nodded to the guard. A shot rang out and the Congolese guard's body fell into the rushing river below.

~

23

Chidi sat on the couch of her laboratory, watching the yellow dot on the screen bounce around in a constant, upward motion. It was Binta, bounding through the jungle, searching for Freya. Chidi held her breath every time the dot paused. It could mean he'd found her, or something got in his way. Every time Binta reached a new elevation, Chidi found herself researching the types of new danger Binta might come across.

She reviewed satellite images taken of the cutoff point where the jungle canopy opened up into pure volcanic rock; it seemed to be the point where bodies disappeared. She'd only heard Howard's campfire stories of the volcano. Freya and Jules pounded it into her head that ninety percent of anything Howard said was an exaggeration, but she suspected some of his stories were at the very least based on truth. Sure, he loved to get a rise out of the girls and his drinking buddies, but she couldn't help but think that his deep respect for the jungle would lend a slight embellishment, not a complete fabrication of the stories he told. Plus, Isolde's lore was pounded into every Congolese child's head from the day they were born. Some of it had to be true.

Logan appeared in the doorway with a man dressed in a park ranger's suit. "This is William. He and his team recovered their fallen ranger. He's in hospital after suffering a gunshot to the chest."

"Ms. Blue, I heard of the troubles with your sister," William said. "I'm so sorry."

Chidi looked at Logan for confirmation. *He doesn't know about Jules and Logan wants to keep it that way.* "And I'm so sorry to hear about Beno."

William clutched his hat to his chest, pressing his fingers into its rim. "I understand that it's all very tenuous, what will happen. We have never had treasure hunters such as these cross our lands. And we don't want to further compromise Freya's position. But the authorities..."

"William, I know that what I'm asking is too much," Chidi said. "Beno's family deserves to know what happened. But I knew Beno. And he would want Freya to survive. I need you to not say anything to the authorities until she returns. I beg of you."

William took in what she was saying. "I respect your predicament, but if I don't follow protocol, more people could get hurt."

"Can you give us a little more time?" Logan asked. "Please."

William stared past them until, resigned, his eyes rose to meet Logan's. "You know where she's going. You know the statistics. I can give you five hours. After that, I must report this to the authorities. I am sorry that I cannot do more for

Freya." William turned to Chidi and grabbed her hand as a show of comfort. Chidi held it back, understanding the gesture to mean that he was sorry for her sister's loss.

24

The midday heat of the jungle was oppressive. Exhaustion fell over Hugo's remaining five guards as they continued the ascent through the thick jungle. It would be another day's trek through the canopy at the volcano's base before they would make it to the porous, rocky cliffs of the volcano itself. It was steep and slow-going, as the guards cut away the foliage of the forgotten path. Freya caught Hugo glancing down at the treacherous path they'd cleared before focusing on the volcano's peak, and wondered if his determination was driving him to madness. That's what happened with most treasure hunters. So sure of themselves, they forget about all the ways they could die.

The higher through the dense jungle they climbed, the more oppressive the humidity became, as evidenced in Hugo and his men, who forced themselves on with each step. Joseph, one of the Congolese guards, stopped and stared ahead until the guard behind shoved him forward.

Joseph stood his ground, his feet firmly planted in place, resisting the urging from his fellow guards. The rest of the group stopped to see what was wrong. After a minute of staring into the jungle, he took one long look at Hugo.

"Bienvenue dans ma montagne."

Welcome to my mountain.

"What?" Hugo asked.

"It's...," Freya uttered. "He said welcome to my mountain."

"Tu vas mourir," Joseph muttered.

Hugo walked over and shook Joseph. "Now is not the time for jokes."

Freya felt the blood rush from her face. "He's gone mad." She'd seen jungle madness before, as a result of oppressive heat, dehydration, or simply rubbing against the wrong type of plant. This was different. It was as though Joseph was possessed.

Albert and the other Congolese guard fell to their knees and prayed.

Hugo turned from Joseph, who was still under the trance. "Tell me what he's saying."

Freya looked at Hugo, ashen. "He's saying that we're going to die."

As the words left her mouth, the ground rolled under Freya's feet, and she and Hugo fell into each other. Freya quickly regained footing and helped Hugo to safety as a crevasse formed beneath them and down the side of the mountain, practically splitting it in two. Tree limbs wavered around them, and they jumped to the same side as Albert as steam rose from the crevasse. She and Hugo grabbed onto a dead tree root as the whole base of the volcano shook and rolled beneath them.

The dead root was quickly pulling away from the muddy

mountainside and sinking into the crack in the ground. Albert helped Hugo to safety. He called for his men to get her before she fell into the crevasse, but the ground rolled underneath them, and they lost their footing. Freya glanced down into the crevasse at what appeared to be bubbling mud and steam rising up beneath her as she sank into it.

The rolling turned into a violent shake, and Freya's body lifted and hit the edge of the sinking tree root over and over. Her arm burned from grasping the root tightly, while her body dangled just above the bubbling dirt and mud below her. She felt her fingers slipping. The mountain shook one last time and her hand released.

She lost her grip and felt the weightlessness of hot air around her until someone grabbed hold of her hand. She glanced up to see Joseph, alert and leaning over the edge of the crevasse, both of his hands wrapped around her forearm. He winced under the strain as he pulled her over the edge of the crevasse to safety. Freya stood in complete shock as Joseph dusted himself off. He smiled, and a second later, the ground gave way beneath his feet and he fell screaming into the crevasse. Freya watched his hand reach through the volcanic, bubbling earth as his screams suddenly ended. The ground shook once more, before the crevasse sealed up before them.

Joseph was gone.

"No!" Freya cried.

Hugo pulled on his pack, staring at the same ground they'd all watched swallow Joseph whole. "Go! Now! Faster. Let's move!"

Freya glanced at the volcano's peak. "We can't. The volcano has been dormant for centuries. I… I… I don't know what you just saw, but clearly it's no longer dormant. The whole valley will be in ashes."

Hugo followed Freya's gaze to the peak. "Time to go. And if anyone mentions that bitch's name, I will gut them from end to end like a fish!" Hugo wiped dirt from his pants and stalked around the crevasse's edge, where Joseph had just fallen to his death.

25

~

They climbed high and tied themselves into trees that night. Freya could hear the Congolese guards conspiring to escape, but they knew they were trapped just like she was. Going back on their agreement to accompany Hugo to the volcano would threaten their families, just like Freya's. Either way, they were on a death march, and their hopelessness was as heavy as the thick jungle air.

Freya glanced up into the canopy and spotted the clear night sky and the twinkling stars. She couldn't shake the images of Joseph's last moments as he sank into the bubbling earth, screaming, before it sealed shut; as though the earth never opened up and Joseph never existed. The threat of an ancient curse always loomed in the background, but Freya and Jules had always laughed those stories off. Had Joseph fallen into the earth? Or was Freya going mad? For the first time, she fully understood Howard's unending respect for the jungle, its history, and inhabitants.

Freya closed her eyes and tried not to self-diagnose

herself as insane. The way things were going, it was just a matter of when and how. She found herself praying. To what, she wasn't sure. *Just keep my family safe.* She imagined that if the curse existed at all, Isolde's pity for her had run out by now. She closed her eyes and leaned her head against the tree trunk. *Not going mad today*, she told herself over and over. Her staunch agnosticism felt oddly comforting. Yet, who could dismiss the day's events? Was it some effect of being this close to Mikeno? Freya thought of all the scientific explanations available to explain what had happened. She convinced herself that they were experiencing some kind of jungle sickness. Joseph was gone, but what she'd seen could not have occurred.

The jungle was alive and awake, despite the setting sun. The oppressive wet heat blurred her vision and made her question what she saw. When she opened her eyes, she felt a fierce lethargy overcome her; as though a great weight held her whole body and thoughts down. She suddenly felt eyes all around her. When she glanced up she saw twinkling irises peeking through the brush. Was it the albino silverback and his pack? Observing their weaknesses, ready to kill them while they slept?

In the trees across from her, Hugo and his men were feeling the same lethargy. They'd passed out from exhaustion. The night sky felt closer than ever. Freya spotted Orion and traced her finger through the Milky Way, Taurus, and Gemini. Howard drilled astronomy into the girls' heads when they were young. They used it to find their way home, if they'd misstepped or taken the wrong path. *Look up. The sky will lead you back*, he liked to say.

I wish you were here, Freya thought. He always found his way out of scrapes. *What should I do now, dad, hmm?*

Howard claimed that he'd nearly entered the volcano

before discovering the abandoned baby Binta. He believed that Isolde had sent him to rescue the gorilla. But the man lived for campfire stories, and his jaded daughters knew he'd taken one too many wrong turns, coupled with far too many sips from his flask. He said that he'd survived the trek because the jungle took pity on him. Freya knew better. The jungle treated invaders like parasites, attacking them until natural order was restored.

Freya snickered at the thought of Howard sitting beside dusty Isolde's bones and having a drink with her from his flask. He was the last person to be interested in riches. He had often said that he lived amongst the riches of the jungle in their tiny little hut, that is, until his wife passed away and his world fell apart.

The sound of a branch rustling snapped Freya back to reality. A set of black eyes moved toward her. She braced herself, then gave in to the thought of death. She recognized the quick snapping of a gorilla bounding through branches and knew it was the silverback. And then she saw a familiar face as he moved close to hers. Binta sniffed her, and she felt the warm grasp of his hand pulling her into him.

"It's you," she whispered.

Freya clung to Binta, who hugged her back and breathed heavily from the exhaustion of his climb. She quickly spotted the tiny tracking device on the inside of his arm. *Chidi.* Freya could only imagine that Binta was sent in the unlikely event they made it to the volcano. Blood dripped from his arm, where a tree limb likely had cut him. *You're hurt,* Freya signed to Binta. She reached for a rubber vine and extracted its milky juice, before wiping away the dried blood with water droplets, and applying the salve to his wound.

Freya come now, Binta signed.

No, I'm going up, Freya signed. *There.* She pointed to the volcano's peak. *Binta come too?*

Binta not go higher, he quickly responded. He grunted softly and pulled away, a rare expression of his discomfort at the thought of a memory he didn't understand, but somehow feared. He stuck to the lowlands, never venturing too high like other gorillas. Howard liked it this way, as he was kept safe. The Blues were his pack. He didn't need to go higher. Freya knew it was something deeper; some survival instinct imprinted in him after his pack abandoned him.

Freya nodded and smiled. At least one of the Blues would survive this. The most sensible one: Binta. She glanced down to find that an exhausted Hugo was barely clinging to the thick tree trunk while his guards slept nearby.

You must hide, Freya signed. She pointed to Hugo and his men. *Bad men with guns. Stay away.*

Binta pulled at her to go with him. When she refused, he took one last look at her before swinging into the tree opposite. The rustling of the branches woke Hugo, and their eyes locked. She turned away and pulled her hoodie up, blocking out the rain. Her body went limp against the tree as exhaustion took hold. She drifted in and out of sleep as the constellations staked their claim in the sky above.

26

The rope held Freya back as she startled awake, and nearly fell twenty feet to the jungle floor. The same couldn't be said for Hugo, who hadn't secured himself well enough to the tree. Tree limbs broke his fall, but they all heard the guttural pain of his smacking against each branch before finally hitting the ground. He clutched his side and breathed heavily before discovering a sharp branch jutting from his side.

After untying herself, Freya pushed through the group surrounding Hugo. He lay on the ground, bleeding out of his side. One of his hands grabbed her wrist. "Help me. Now." He bit down on a stick and clutched two thick branches. Blood ran from his side, and his face grew pale.

"Get me the alcohol and a wrap," she said.

Albert quickly handed her the items as she looked on either side of her to Hugo's men. They instinctually understood her and pinned Hugo down.

Freya poured alcohol over the wound, then removed the stick so he could take a drink. Seconds later she reached down and pulled the branch from his side. He screamed in pain as his men held him as still as possible, and Freya pressed the bandage against his wound, wrapping the rest quickly around his waist.

"Congratulations on your first Congo surgery." Pitiless, Freya wiped her hands and walked away. "Everyone get your things together. We climb in two minutes."

Freya glanced at the peak, which loomed directly overhead. She couldn't help but think: *the jungle is doing a number on him. What's in store for me?*

Two of Hugo's men helped him climb until he pushed them off and was overcome by some unforeseen energy. Short of a miracle, it would be mere hours before he bled out unless Freya did something to stop the bleeding. His face was ashen but determined. He grabbed a nearby walking stick, pushed his men away, and attempted to keep up with Freya, grunting with each effort.

"We'll need to stop soon. Stitch you up. You're losing too much blood."

Hugo's strained breathing had turned to a wheeze. He continued climbing and said, "You know, I think part of you wants to find the treasure as much as I do."

Freya scoffed. "If I wanted to find it, I would've done so by now."

Hugo laughed before choking and spitting up some blood. He smiled, his teeth stained red. "I know you. You need to break rules or you will die. Just like me."

"We are nothing alike."

"I know it's getting to you." He coughed up more blood. "Her. The treasure. Just wait until the diamond is staring you in the face and you fall under its spell and then tell me you don't want it."

It was then that Freya spotted it and abruptly stopped. Hugo ran into her and collapsed. Freya and Albert picked him up.

Freya pointed it out to the group: the first real trap of the volcano. One of many, she suspected, in the form of a poison plant. The ibogaine plant blocked a large part of the path. Though she rarely came across it in the lowlands, it thrived in the rich volcanic soil and appeared to surround them. It was jungle 101 to avoid poisonous plants; drilled into every kid in the DRC from birth. She pointed it out and wrapped herself and Hugo with a blanket as they walked through it.

"It's sweltering," he cried. The huge dark rings under his eyes and his pale face hinted that the end was near for him. They would have to stop soon or he wouldn't make it.

"Don't touch it, unless you do want to go mad," Freya said, smacking his hand away and pointing at the plant, which crowded most of the path as far as she could see. "Which, in your case, might be an improvement." She turned and stalked through the plant, dodging it with every step.

Two of Hugo's remaining five men took machetes to clear the path. Tiny orange pepper-like bulbs swung to the ground as the group avoided them with great care. Still, Freya felt a branch graze her exposed ankle. She sighed and closed her eyes momentarily. Even the slightest exposure would send its victim reeling into madness.

"C'a m'a touches," one of Hugo's men uttered after being grazed by the plant.

"If we pick up the pace, we'll get through this." Freya couldn't tell if the heatwave that overcame her was a result of the blanket covering her, or the effects of the plant. "We'll have to stop soon. Let the effects wear off."

The men ahead sped up their process of clearing the bushes, which seemed to multiply the higher they climbed. She looked through a clearing that appeared in the canopy above. The sun sat mid-sky and blazing. It shone down on the tip of the volcano and exposed a slight trail of smoke that emitted from its peak. She learned as a young girl that the volcano never truly rested. It released some kind of gases or heat at all times of the day.

She looked up again as they moved closer to the side of the volcano. Though it was mere moments later, the sun appeared to have moved west, its rays slightly blocked by the volcano's peak. *How could that be?* Freya thought. They were in the same place on the trail. How could they be in the same place?

They were exhausted and had fierce heat rashes, just like the rest of the group, when Hugo's lone British guard, sick with madness, burst through and ran into the bushes. He pressed his way through the leaves and innocent-looking orange bulbs, disregarding Freya's warning about touching the plant.

"Where is he going?" Hugo watched in disbelief as the guard pressed through, away from the group and the trail itself. "Stop him!"

Albert and the last two Congolese guards stood still as the man in the middle of the orange bulbs screamed in madness.

Freya turned to Hugo. "There's nothing we can do for him."

The guard sank into the middle of the orange bulbs, which, from Freya's affected point of view, appeared to close in on him.

Freya rubbed her brow. Her vision blurred. "We have to move. Quickly. Get to a safe place where we can let the effects wear off." Despite the man's continued screams, she continued through the clearing.

It was then that Freya's eyes rolled into the back of her head. Two guards ran to her aid as her body went limp. The jungle canopy spun above, and the blazing afternoon light faded to black. "Tie me up," Freya heard herself say out loud. She reached in her satchel for some of the rubber vine and handed it to Albert. "Put some of this on his wound and stitch him up."

"She's gone mad," Hugo said.

"Tie us all up," Freya ordered. "Quickly. If you want to live." Hugo's guards tied them all to surrounding trees so that they wouldn't wander into the bushes in their madness.

Freya closed her eyes as the jungle spun around her. She went in and out of consciousness, once waking to see Hugo and his men getting sick before her. Their bodies were purging the poison, a good sign. She felt panic as she saw a group of insects and spiders crawl toward her. They started on her ankle, some slithering up her pant leg. She stopped herself from itching her body.

"It's not real," she whispered to herself. She woke, crying from the desire to scratch the skin from her body. She turned her head to the side and saw a massive white spider sitting on the tree trunk. Its black eyes stared her down. "You want to kill me. But you're not real."

She thought she heard groans from Hugo and his men, but she couldn't tell if it was a hallucination.

"Nothing you see is real," Freya said to them. "It's a hallucination."

But madness overtook one of the remaining guards. He

escaped his bonds and ran, quickly losing his footing, rolling down the mountain and careening off the edge.

"Such a pity," a familiar voice said.

Freya glanced up and saw none other than Howard sitting cross-legged before her. In her hallucination he was sober, a strange and unlikely memory.

Freya smiled. "Papa."

"You're still getting into scrapes, aren't you, my girl?"

"I didn't want to. You know that."

He smiled. "Part of me believes you."

"Jules. I have to save her."

"From this mountain top? Whether your sister realizes it yet or not, she can save herself."

"She's gone soft. Lived in the city too long."

Howard smiled. "She's made of the same hearty stuff as you, city or no."

"Will I survive this?" Freya asked with a laugh.

"I think that maybe Hugo has a point. You want to make it to that mountain peak as much as I did in my living days," Howard said.

"Are you implying that I have the same sickness as you?"

"How far do you think you'll go?" Howard turned and looked at the volcano's peak.

"You didn't answer my question," Freya said, closing and reopening her eyes to make sure he was still there.

"I daresay you'll make it," Howard said. "Provided your brother makes the journey."

"He doesn't want to go," Freya said.

Suddenly, Binta came bounding up. He nuzzled into Howard's side and pulled him into his chest.

"Hello, my boy," Howard said. "I've missed you so." Howard held Binta's face in his hands. "You're going to have to help your sister now. Do you hear me?" It was clear that Binta understood everything Howard was saying. He sighed and closed his watery eyes before pressing his face into Howard's shoulder. Freya imagined Binta thinking how wonderful it would be if they could all just swing through the trees and return to Chidi. Howard received Binta's embrace and hugged him close. He pulled some berries out of his pocket. "Eat these, both of you. They'll lessen the effects of the plant. Make you right again."

Binta picked up two of the chunky blue berries often found in a cooler climate of the opposing mountains and nibbled them. Freya vaguely recalled Chidi stuffing them in her pocket before she left, but the memory flashed and was gone. She grabbed some and popped them in her mouth.

Howard loosened the ropes around Freya's hands. Binta crawled beside Freya and leaned against the tree, his eyes still glassy from the effects of the plant. A clearness came over her as the mysterious berries took hold and brought her back to reality. *Get to the treasure. Save your sisters.*

"I must go now," Howard said. "There's something I need to remind you of before I go. The diamond must stay in the volcano. It belongs to her."

Freya pointed to Hugo, or where she thought she could see him, anyway. "He wants it."

Howard briefly glanced at Hugo before turning back to Freya and Binta. "It is not his to take." And just like that, he flashed his mischievous smile and disappeared.

Freya noticed the clearing as soon as Howard was gone. In the place of the hallucinogenic plants stood palm trees and innocent jungle flowers.

"Thank you, Papa." Freya rubbed her eyes and pushed herself up as Hugo and his men slowly came to.

As she sat up there was a figure rushing through the brush toward her. She smiled, remembering that Binta was likely nearby. But the figure didn't stop. It rushed toward her at full speed until it came into full view. It wasn't Binta at all. Before her, rearing up and baring his teeth in an earsplitting roar, was the Albino silverback.

27

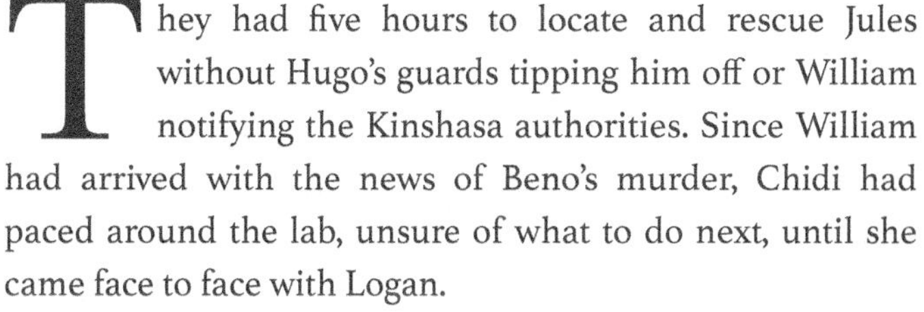

They had five hours to locate and rescue Jules without Hugo's guards tipping him off or William notifying the Kinshasa authorities. Since William had arrived with the news of Beno's murder, Chidi had paced around the lab, unsure of what to do next, until she came face to face with Logan.

"You need to ground yourself," he said.

"Ground myself!" Chidi pounded her fist on the counter.

"This isn't a time to freak out."

Chidi felt frantic. "We've limited time to locate Jules and if we don't move fast she'll be killed, but if we move too fast, Hugo finds out and Freya's dead. And Jules could be... anywhere. You saw... she's in some dark basement."

After observing the scene like the child of warring parents, Sascha stood and raised his hand. "You know, I am pretty handy with geolocation, and all that..."

"What?" Chidi glanced from Sascha to Logan and back.

"I can find her," Sascha said, glancing around the room for errant wild animals. "Probably."

"You can?"

Logan shook his head. "No way. You cannot get involved in this. Your board is blowing up my phone."

"Fuck the board," Sascha said, kicking the ground.

Chidi knew Logan worked for tech industry higher-ups, but it was becoming clearer that Sascha had a lot of handlers searching for him. "He has a... board? Who is he?"

Logan rolled his eyes. "Do you read the news? I mean, do you even check the internet?"

"I do, I just tend to stay on scientific websites," Chidi responded.

Logan was about to give him another excuse, but Sascha cut him off. "Just let me help. Please? And then I'll do whatever you want."

Chidi turned to Logan, pleading. "I'm not sure why you're hesitating, but if he can find her, then bloody well let him help. At least *one* of my sisters should survive this catastrophe."

Logan stared at the ground, balled his fists and groaned, shutting his eyes to the scene before exhaling and returning to the moment. "Chidi, get him a computer. Not yours—we don't want anything traced back to you. See if that guard had one in his satchel."

"I think he may have communicated with Hugo on an old laptop," Chidi responded. "I'll find it."

"Good." Logan turned to Sascha. "And you. After you locate Jules, *if* you locate her, we're dropping you at the airfield and you're getting on a plane back to California. I'll secure a car and driver to get you there. And when you get back, you tell your board you decided to fanny off to Monaco for some gambling. You understand?"

"I'm not allowed one hundred feet near any casinos in the whole world, so that wouldn't jive," Sascha said.

"What?" Chidi was incredulous. Each of Sascha's confessions added to his mystery.

Logan wiped his brow. "Right. I forgot. Well make something up that your board will believe and that won't be traced back to me. Otherwise, you're funding my early retirement because you broke the terms of our contract and willfully put yourself in trouble." He turned to Chidi. "The laptop? We're running out of time."

Chidi was staring at the scene before she snapped back to reality. "Right."

When she returned with the laptop, Sascha was knee deep in the storage room, unearthing Howard's ancient technology that she couldn't bring herself to part with. Logan was searching the property for any of the guards' weapons they could take with them to Kinshasa.

"You know you can tell him to sod off about the computers," Chidi said.

Sascha jumped from underneath a dusty old tarp and hit his head. "Oh god. You scared me."

"Logan probably needs you more than you need him."

"You would think that," Sascha said. "But it seems to be the other way around." He chuckled as he tapped a filthy tube attached to a massive machine that spanned the length of the storage room. "You know, this is really special. I've only ever seen ENIACS in museums. Never up close like this."

Chidi laughed. "Papa liked to collect broken down machines and tinker with them. This one has been collecting dust for the better part of twenty years. In fact, be careful. There might be a family of meerkats in there somewhere."

"Howard and I would've gotten along swimmingly," Sascha said, smiling.

"I'm afraid you won't find my sister with that thing." Chidi pulled out the laptop used by Hugo's guard. "I suspect he's still signed on to my network and that's why Freya and Jules are still alive. They think we're just sitting here in wait."

Sascha sat at Chidi's desk, fired up the laptop, and cracked his knuckles before overriding the security within seconds. "And they shall continue to think so."

Chidi watched as Sascha mined the laptop for information of Jules' whereabouts. He noticed a communication the day prior with a network in Kinshasa and pinpointed its location.

Logan walked in and observed the map highlighting the Kinshasa warehouse location.

"Hmm, hmm," Logan said before walking away.

"Oh, come on now, you stubborn fool," Chidi said, placing her hands on Sascha's shoulders. "Without your friend tagging along, we would have never located Jules. Can't you thank him?"

"You just called him a fool, and he doesn't have you in a headlock," Sascha said.

Logan's phone chimed. "Ah, perfect timing. Thank you, Sascha. Your driver is here to take you to the airport. He's been verified by my network, so I feel comfortable releasing you into his care. He'll get you to the airfield safely."

"Understood, boss," Sascha said. "Hmm, I've never had a boss. This feels so weird. Thanks for the, uh... little adventure. I will see you when you get back home."

"Check in with your board as soon as you take off," Logan said as Sascha waved and left the room. "They're all shitting themselves."

Chidi turned to Logan. "So who is he now?"

Logan rolled his eyes, pulled on his pack. "Let's focus on getting Jules back."

Chidi followed Logan outside and locked up the lab.

Logan threw his pack in the back seat of the jeep and checked the safety on the weapon he'd found on the dead guard. "It doesn't matter who he is as long as he makes it home safe."

"You seem genuinely worried," Chidi said, following Logan out. "As though he's your friend."

"Just drop it," Logan said. "We have to focus. We have a location, but no idea how many guards are around this compound."

"I do want to hear about the casino bit another time, though." Satisfied with her ribbing, Chidi caught up to Logan at the jeep, and they started their journey to Kinshasa.

~

28

Freya opened her eyes and felt her grip release from the tree. She couldn't shake the feeling of the albino silverback rushing toward her, rearing up, and sinking his teeth into her neck. Every part of her knew that this vision was a preview of what was to come. He was gigantic, as though the centuries had built his frame into the black volcano's opposite; an indestructible creature built of blood and ice. The image of his entranced red eyes focused on her alone was seared into her brain. He was waiting for her to step foot on his turf, so he could take the first and only swipe needed to end her.

Hugo stood with a surprising vigor as his guards slowly recovered from the trance. He peeled back the bandage where his wound was. To Freya's surprise, the milk from the rubber plant had provided a surprising salve and his wound looked as though it was healing. His cheeks looked flushed and healthy, as though some kind of miracle cure had been applied.

"You look like you've seen a ghost," he said, chuckling. "It's time to get going."

Freya was dumbfounded. It was as though the volcano had worked some kind of miracle cure on Hugo, while filling her with a debilitating dread. Howard's answer to her quandary resounded in her head. *Isolde is fattening him up for the slaughter.* She pushed herself to standing and faltered a bit before joining the group.

They found a small stream, filled their casks, and drank as though they'd walked through a desert. Hugo tracked her every movement, flaunting his renewed energy at every step. He barked orders at his guards, who were still dizzy from the toxic brush they'd passed through.

Freya peered up at the top of the volcano for what seemed like the hundredth time. Grey smoke polluted the blue sky, as though a lightning storm was brewing. The noxious smell of volcanic gases rose from the black, porous rock as they started their ascent. They were close. Surely closer than anyone had ever been to Isolde and her treasure. Freya spotted the jagged cliffs of the long-dormant volcano. Jet black rock jutted out in diamond formations on the side, as though Isolde had created makeshift lookout points before throwing treasure hunters to their deaths.

The more she peered upward, the more her view was obscured by a dense fog that appeared from out of nowhere. It obscured their view. They could barely see two steps in front of them. One misstep and any number of them could be sent careening off the side of the volcano.

Hugo joined at her side. "Now is no time for fear, Freya Blue. Why are you stopping?"

She caught his gaze and once again spotted his determined lust for the diamond that clearly overpowered common sense. Common sense that might keep them from dying.

He nudged her forward.

Howard's words rang in her ears as she took one careful step after another. *The diamond stays in the volcano.* Was there even a diamond? And if she made it to the volcano, what was she considering? Was it the madness affecting her? How could she keep her sisters safe and attend to the whims of her father's ghost? She glanced up and found herself asking for help. There was no response, as expected, so she continued on, her mind paralyzed at the myriad disasters that might befall them next. The rocky path up the jagged side of the volcano narrowed and the jungle canopy sat just below them. Freya glanced down just as her foot slipped.

"What on earth..." The volcanic black rock she'd tread moments before had transformed into a slick sheet of ice. Her stomach dropped as the glacier came into full view and she felt the immediate intensity of the cold on her skin. Clouds of condensation filled the air with every exhale; something she'd never experienced in the Congo. She glanced ahead and could see that the blackened sheet of ice was covered in hard snow and spanned a quarter of the mountainside.

"I said keep going!" Hugo's temper overtook him as his foot slipped on the black ice, and he fell, gripping the side of the volcano for support. The two guards surrounding him slipped, and one nearly fell over the side.

"It's... it's turned to ice," Freya called out. "Get your ropes, anything you can use to secure yourself."

"You heard her." Hugo took the knife from its sheath and launched it into the side of the icy mountain. He pulled himself along step by step with a new determination. "Get moving! And you will be rewarded. Anyone who helps me get to the treasure gets to fill their pockets with as much gold as they can handle."

The three guards fumbled in their packs with a new urgency, the promise of wealth making the treachery they faced seem like a minor inconvenience. Freya took out a gripping hook and rope. She tied the rope around her waist and held tight to the side of the mountain, using her hook to move her along. Hugo and his guards followed behind, some slipping on ice and grabbing on to each other.

The fog thickened the further they ascended the volcano. Freya shivered but forced her frostbitten fingers to remove the gripping hook and launch it in repeatedly. The temperature continued to drop as they moved to the midpoint of the glacier. One man slipped and lost his footing. Another guard caught him, but not without setting off a domino of the group fumbling around for their footing, and nearly dropping off the side of the glacier.

It was then that Freya felt it. A sudden, strong, swift wash of air, as though a creature ran past and was trying to knock her off the side of the mountain. She heard the whizzing sound again. The men felt it brush their sides as well.

"What is that?" Albert cried.

"Keep going! Just keep going!" Freya continued, her gripping hook clanging against the black ice of the volcano. She stopped and pressed her back against the mountainside when the creature brushed past again. The fog remained thick. She couldn't identify the creature, but she had a sick feeling in her stomach that she knew exactly what it was.

"It's trying to knock us off," she whispered to herself.

Freya turned her body forward and launched the hook into the ice. It was then that she saw it. A brief flash of relief was quickly followed by a new sense of fear as she watched a massive cassowary bird speed past her. She'd only heard of the native birds, but never seen one face to face. The stories of their viciousness were proving true.

One of Hugo's guards cried out as the bird bit into his side, before disappearing again into the fog. The guard lost his footing and slipped down the side of the mountain, disappearing from view with little more than a single cry of pain. Another bird sped past them, this time using its talon to swipe at Freya's arm. She looked down and saw the blood pouring from her bicep.

"Fast now! As fast as you can go," she called. "Use your hooks to swipe at the birds, if you can."

Freya plodded forward, one step at a time, swiping her hook at any approaching cassowaries. She turned to see Albert usher Hugo ahead, as the other guard caught a cassowary with his hook. Stunned, the powerful bird clawed at his face, and the two fell to their deaths. There was no reason for the bird to be at this altitude.

Freya saw the clearing ahead and stepped onto the volcanic gravel. Almost immediately, the bitter fog was replaced by a sweltering mist. She went from shivering to sweating. To her great, if momentary, relief, the screaming cries of the cassowaries died out. She turned around and saw Hugo and Albert clear the glacier. A cassowary had clawed the side of Hugo's face. He somehow appeared even stronger the more the volcano threw at him.

He glanced at her and wiped the blood away with his forearm. "Is that all she's got?"

Freya would've liked to think they'd made it through the worst, but her instincts told her that was naïve thinking. The vivid image of the albino silverback hadn't left her mind. She didn't doubt that he was waiting for her. She glanced back toward the glacier and found that the ice had disappeared, replaced by the same volcanic rock on which she was standing.

"It's gone..."

Freya fell to the ground and glanced up at the peak. Something was blocking her view. The albino silverback was standing at the crest of the volcano, staring directly at her.

"You're really there. Or am I losing my mind?"

Even from this distance, she could see the red veins in his eyes. It almost made them glow. As her eyes focused on the sight, she realized he wasn't alone. His pack appeared behind him, ready for battle.

29

Logan and Chidi were halfway to Kinshasa when the jeep hit a huge pothole and they heard a cry coming from under the tarp. Logan pulled to the side of the road. He knew that voice; the one that had been both plaguing and growing oddly endearing to him in Palo Alto. He lifted the tarp to find Sascha very carefully hiding between two spare tires.

Logan had to turn away to keep from screaming. His foot stamped the ground as he tried to conceal his anger from Chidi. He shook his arms and took a deep breath before turning around. Sascha pushed himself up, but not before Logan started toward him.

"Why?" Logan said, fuming. "Why didn't you follow directions? That was the deal!"

Sascha froze. "I felt like... you might need some backup," he said, pulling a stuck foot from between a tire. "Though you might not know it, I have driven a car, and I can be the getaway guy. You know?" It took one look at Logan for

Sascha to understand that he was in trouble. “And I know we… we discussed me getting on the plane, but, but…”

“Get in the back seat and call your damn board,” Logan said. He opened the door and Sascha shrunk into the back seat. “And buckle the hell up.”

“TONDON,” Chidi said, looking at her phone. “I know who you are now. You invented the democratic, like free rights…”

“Search engine,” Sascha said, smiling.

“That,” Chidi said, smiling and pointing at him.

“I promise to fix your computer when we get back—”

“Nope,” Logan quipped. “You’re getting on a plane. I’m going to strap you in myself. Get a big muscled guy to keep you in your damn seat.” He started up the engine, and they were back on the freeway in a few seconds, the busy Kinshasa traffic surrounding them.

“New plan,” Logan said, donning some aviators. “I go in and get Jules. You stay with this one.”

“That’s really not necessary,” Sascha said. “I’m here for support.”

“Too late for that,” Logan said. “You’ve put yourself in the middle of rescuing someone from armed kidnappers. This is exactly the kind of scenario you pay me to help you avoid. If they find out you’re with us, they will quickly kill Jules and go after you for a huge ransom.”

Sascha sat back in his seat, deflated. “I didn’t think about that. That’s why you told me to—”

Logan cut him off. “Get on a plane and go home. That’s right. But did you listen? No. You never do.”

“This is an unusual business relationship,” Chidi said.

“Deep down, I know Logan loves me,” Sascha said. “He just has a funny way of expressing it.”

She snickered and lowered her glasses, glancing at

Logan, who smiled defeatedly.

They arrived in central Kinshasa. Cars and trucks kicked up dust around them. The afternoon heat hit them as they made it to the warehouse district and arrived at the location that Sascha pinpointed on Hugo's server. Logan parked a block away and observed the scene. The warehouse was surrounded by a massive fence with security cameras at every corner and entrance.

"They'll see us. There, there." Chidi pointed out the numerous cameras displaying the building surroundings. "How will you get in? Wait, I think I've got an idea."

A minute later, Chidi was at the entrance, buzzing the doorbell.

A voice came over the loudspeaker. "What do you need?"

"Hello," Chidi said. "I'm here for my two o'clock fitting. Bernard sent me."

"You have the wrong building," the voice echoed back.

Chidi rattled off the address, glancing at a sheet of paper. "I really need your help. This is the building, I just know it. Let me call my agent, one sec."

Seconds later, the gate opened, and a guard walked out. "You have the wrong building. You need to move along."

"That can't be. Bernard told me to be here to meet the designer. What building are you talking about? Do you mind showing me?" Chidi led him out to the street, where Logan was in wait. Before the guard knew it, Logan pulled him into the bushes and knocked him out. He took the guard's walkie talkie and keys and quickly responded to the radio query from the other guard on the inside of the compound.

Chidi returned to the car and got in. Sascha's face surfaced from under the tarp.

"I guess that was hard for you, pretending to be a model," Sascha said. "I still think that I could've convincingly pulled it off, but I understand Logan's hesitation."

"Logan wanted me to remind you that you're a valuable target," Chidi said. "He asked that you resist your urge to help and please don't do anything dumb. So is he like your dad or something?"

Sascha concealed his face again. "I'm not ready to talk about family dynamics, but basically, yes. I resent him saying those things. I'm working on my compulsions."

Chidi tapped her fingers on the dash, impatiently waiting for Logan to appear with Jules. They'd waited in the jeep for over thirty minutes and Chidi was restless. She stared at the radio before pressing herself into her seat. "He should be back by now. Something is up."

"Isn't he like a trained Navy SEAL or something?" Sascha asked.

"Something like that. But he doesn't have any backup." Chidi got out of the jeep. "I'm going in."

Sascha shot up. "N... no. You can't go in. He said you need to stay here."

"Get down," Chidi said. "Do what Logan says. If we're not out in thirty minutes, take the jeep to the nearest airfield and call your board. You do not want these people knowing you're here." With that, Chidi donned a ball cap and darted around the corner.

Sascha sat for twenty minutes with nothing but an old French radio to listen to. It wasn't until he heard a big crash from inside the warehouse that he jumped out of the jeep and hesitantly walked toward the side entrance where Chidi had entered.

~

30

Freya couldn't figure out what was real and what was imagined. After spotting the albino silverback overhead and nearly dying from the glacier and cassowary attack, all she could do was close her eyes. When she did, he was still there, rearing up to attack her. *Is this how treasure hunters go mad?* She deduced that they had nowhere to look but down, and inevitably just fell to their deaths.

Hugo was down to one guard—Albert—who had somehow deflected the cassowaries' attacks. The three of them leaned against the side of the volcano and slid to the ground, catching their breath. But it was nearly impossible with the gaseous winds blowing past, the strong sulfuric smell of rotten eggs filling the air. There was just enough space on the path to sit with their knees up to their chests.

As she closed her eyes, she recalled a figure that appeared in her dream just before Howard. It was a white spider as large as Hugo's tallest guard. It walked on its massive legs through the group and straight toward Freya before turning and enveloping one of Hugo's men in its grasp. Still alive, he stared straight into the beast's black eyes, before pleading with Freya to save him.

She cast the vision out of her mind and opened her eyes. Albert sat beside her. His body completely still, he gazed at her as the white spider from her dream—this one much smaller, but just as poisonous—crawled up his face. Albert had already been bitten and appeared to be paralyzed from the neck down. Freya gasped and looked around frantically for something to knock it off. Before she could find anything, she heard him mouth the words 'aides-moi,' only seconds before the spider latched on and launched its poison into Albert's eye. His head shook, and the spider scurried away. The color drained from Albert's face. Freya took his pulse.

It was too late.

Hugo woke and jumped at the sight of Albert's dead body beside him. Freya stood and held out her hand to Hugo.

Freya faced Hugo head on. "Whatever is in store for us, I promise you. It will be ten times worse. This is our last chance to turn around. We will die if we keep going." *And we will probably die if we turn back*, she thought, but didn't say aloud.

Hugo smiled. It seemed that the further he climbed, the stronger his desire became. "What's worse? You dying? Or you and your sisters dying? I plan to live. Hmm?" He stepped around her before stopping. "I forgot—you're leading this excursion. Why don't you go ahead?"

The resounding echo of the albino silverback's roar rang out over the edge of the volcano base. Without Binta, they wouldn't make it anywhere near the entrance. She and her sisters were as good as dead.

"Ready?" Freya asked. "This is what you wanted, isn't it?" She turned and started ascending the final peak of the mountainside. Clarity overcame her as she ascended, as though the worst of the curse was over. And then the realization hit her. *I'm not here to help Hugo. I'm here to help Isolde.*

31

They climbed over a ridge to find a flat expanse before them. The black rock gave way to rich black soil with sparse, baby trees dotted around the peak. Through a rare break in the clouds and fog, Freya saw the full expanse of the parklands and jungle below them. She heard Howard's voice in her ear. *The soil near the volcano is the richest in the world. Find some of it, and you can plant anything.* Freya knelt down and felt the dirt. It was practically glistening.

After getting her bearings, Freya finally spotted the entrance to the volcano and Isolde's final resting place. Centuries before, her tribe had created an opening in the side of the volcano and covered it with a rock door, allowing her spirit body free movement to and from the tomb. It was covered in an overgrowth of thick, spiky vines.

Freya imagined a royal procession, centuries old, one where Isolde and her daughter unwittingly were carried to a safe place for their eternal rest. Now it was nothing but a treasure hunt for looters and adventure seekers. It was clear that no one had made it this far. Maybe Isolde was tired and needed someone to shut the doors on her final resting place forever. Freya felt as though she'd been unwittingly selected to finish the job.

Hugo plodded past her. He seemed taller than before; the climb invigorating and not depleting him. He stopped abruptly as the silverback's family appeared around the barren edges of the volcano's peak.

"Lower your eyes. Don't move." Freya gazed at the ground as the silverback came into view.

Hugo gasped as he peered straight up at the silverback before his gaze shot down to the ground. The ground started to shake beneath them. The silverback approached him and let out a deafening roar that echoed so loudly, Birds flew from the canopy beneath them. The jungle then fell silent as the king of the volcano reared up and pounded his chest. His pack closed in around Freya and Hugo.

In an instant, the silverback launched at Hugo, but was met midair by Binta, who shoved Hugo aside. The ground shook violently as Binta struggled to overtake the gorilla that had abandoned him at the start of his life. The silverback stopped and stared at Binta, his jaw going slack for a minute as he took his orphan son in. He shook his grey head and moments later bared his teeth before biting into Binta's shoulder.

Binta writhed and screamed in pain before freeing himself. Immediately, another gorilla launched into him. Before Freya could gather what was happening, she saw the silverback's pack, one after another, attack Binta. Binta was on the ground, underneath two others, screaming in pain.

The path to the inside of the volcano began to crack open beneath her feet. "If you don't protect him, I won't protect you," Freya said to the air. She pleaded with Isolde, the ghost queen she'd refused to believe in.

The ground shook violently again, before one final explosion shook the two gorillas from Binta and freed him. He stood in a defensive position as three others closed in on him. Freya noticed that the glassy look in his eye was overtaking him. The silverback rebounded and parted the sea of his pack that was closing in on Binta. He let out a growl of acknowledgement. *Join us, or die*, it seemed to say.

Binta growled in response, weary from the fight. He shook his head, as though trying to shake the trance and save Freya. He stalked toward the silverback and the pack surrounded him. *He's lost*, Freya thought. Then the ground shook and loosed the curse from Binta, who was face to face with the entire pack. The silverback recognized his adversary once more, though Freya noted a look of resignation in his eye. Binta was his blood. And now he had to fight him.

Binta turned and tore into one of the gorillas, before launching it into the group and unsettling them. The pack attacked, and Freya watched as the brother she'd known her whole life fought off one after another, badly wounding some, while throwing others off the cliff. It was a strength she'd never seen in him before.

As Binta fought off one attacker after another, Freya noticed the looming presence approaching her. The silverback faced her. The entrance was so close she could see it through the thick haze. *Should we make a run for it? She pushed off the thought as pure madness.* There was no way to get around the silverback and his pack.

Volcanic explosions rocked the earth beneath them. Hugo pressed his body against the volcano wall and slid his body slowly toward the entrance, clearly trying not to get the attention of the pack. He took out his machete, preparing to cut away the vines near the entrance.

The silverback bared his teeth at Freya and reared, attracting Binta's focus. He jumped the silverback just as Freya was about to be mauled. The two grappled close to the edge while smoke rose around them and the ground shook. This was Freya's chance. She looked to the sky, demanding protection for Binta. Isolde would have to sacrifice something for her, as well.

"Now!" Freya said.

She and Hugo ran toward the entrance. They cut through the overgrown vines and, using all their energy, uncovered the stone entrance to Isolde's final resting place. Freya squeezed through the opening and Hugo followed.

Freya glanced outside the opening, where Binta still faced off with the silverback. Both of them looked weak from the struggle, but battled on. It was as though the silverback had forgotten his final task; to protect the entrance to the volcano at all costs. His desire to control his own family had taken over.

Volcanic gases filled Freya's view, and bits of rock fell around them. She saw Binta lay a massive blow to the silverback before her view was obscured by the rock.

32

~

Logan made his way to a neon-lit basement hallway. The walls were concrete, which explained why his signal had been weak. Something kicked on inside of him, and the flashbacks came. With each step on the hardened concrete, he heard his steps inside the compound of the long-sought after terrorist his SEAL team had hunted. The man was closely associated with the Bin Laden family and had played an integral role in the bombing of the World Trade Center. He had managed to evade every international force tracking him down; the CIA, MI6, BND, Mossad, and more. That is, until, with the help of MI6, Logan's team was directed to the remote location in Afghanistan where he was hiding out.

The echoes of each step took him back to that place; the dry, incessant heat of the afternoon sun reflecting off of cracks in the windows, the arid breeze, the cry of a hungry mutt from the dirt road surrounding the compound. It all came back to him in the dark light of the Kinshasa basement. Logan feared there was little chance that Jules was still alive. If Freya had even helped them scale half the mountain, Hugo or his men had likely killed her by now. And that would mean Jules was extra weight, with no value. Still, something told him to plod on. They'd seen activity coming from the opposite side of the building. There was still a small chance that Jules was alive, which meant Freya was also still alive. Despite their separation, the thought of Freya not being in his ether any longer sent pangs through his body. They'd been together for so long, and even in their separation, had remained the best of friends. He knew Freya's time was limited; one risk she took or another would take her away from him. Still, he wasn't prepared for the thought to even cross his mind.

A clang from down the hall forced him to dart across the hallway for cover. Moments later, an exhausted-looking guard shuffled past his view. An automatic weapon hung at his side, the safety off. He heard the man exchange words in French with another guard, who was out of Logan's view. Their tone raised and the exchange quickly ended. The man shuffled back, carrying a mess plate with slop over the sides. The clang had likely been Jules knocking something over, Logan imagined.

He inched down the hallway once more, cognizant of the echoes he made this time. He gripped his weapon, aware of the tightness of his fingers. *Relax, flow*, he thought. *Remember the flow.* He and his team had been trained in such a way that their steps, every movement, flowed like air, like water, with a freedom not associated with mounting an attack. He fell into it, adopting a lightness he hadn't felt in years. His commander was all about marrying meditation with a mission; being in the zone, blending in. Here, Logan was blending into the hardness of his environment, just like he had back in Afghanistan. There, he had witnessed atrocities he'd tried to drink away. The rest of life was holding it together, trying to form relationships again, or keep the ones he had.

After Afghanistan, his marriage to Freya fell apart. It was his doing, and he knew it. They both had a familiarity with the drink, but he allowed himself to fall into it, despite her years-long efforts to pull him out of a depression he wasn't aware he had. Before he realized it, it was too late. Freya was gone to England to be with Jules and had sent him divorce papers. Still, he held tight to the belief that their bond was for life, even if their marriage wasn't. So here he was, across the world, willing to do anything for his family.

He passed by the security room, where another guard was sacked out. It was there he saw Chidi on one of the screens. *Of course*, he thought to himself. Give a Blue sister a mission and she does the opposite. Out of all the Blue sisters, he expected more of Chidi, but she still had the Blue 'go get 'em' attitude Howard had instilled in them all. He stepped into the security room, covered the guard's mouth, and knocked him out by pressing into a point on his neck. The man went limp and Logan lowered him to the ground. He tied him up and took his weapon. Next, he disarmed the security gates and doors, then determined where Jules was being kept. He had only moments before the guards outside noticed something was up. He turned off the cameras and checked the hallway before moving at a brisk clip. He was close.

"Arrete," the guard said. It was the one Logan had heard yelling from before. But now he had his weapon trained at Logan. The guard in front of Jules' door jumped up and also pointed his gun at Logan. Logan lowered his gun to the ground and raised his hands, smiling.

"J'ai pris un mauvais virage," Logan said, joking about a wrong turn.

The guard behind him forced him to the ground and started binding his wrists, but Logan flipped him over, grabbed his weapon, and took out the second guard, who was about to shoot. The guard on the ground was yelling, but Logan placed the rag at his side in his mouth to shut him up and bound him. The guard writhed on the floor as Logan grabbed his keys and unlocked the door to Jules' room.

Inside, Jules was tied to a metal chair, her hands bloody from being that way for days. Her head drooped, and for a moment, Logan was sure she was dead. Her face was ashen, her eyes surrounded by dark circles. He lifted her chin.

"Jules?"

Her eyes opened, but just barely. She was clearly dehydrated and couldn't speak or eat. He lifted a canister of water to her lips.

"Drink."

Water spilled down her lips, but she was able to swallow some of it. "Is that you?"

Logan cut her wrists free, and her body went limp. He caught her and picked her up. "Let's get you out of here."

"Where are we?"

"Kinshasa."

"Get me..." Her voice trailed off.

Logan set her down. "Jules? Jules, stay with me. I need you awake." He lightly smacked her face.

"Back to London," she whispered.

"Anything for you. And a strong martini. Okay? Just stay with me." Logan carried her down the concrete hallway, one hand clutching his handgun.

"I told Freya you were too good for her."

"Yeah, well. She didn't believe you."

A door busted open. Logan rested Jules against the side of the wall and pointed his gun at the door, ready to fire. Chidi busted through the other side, followed by a shaken Sascha. Chidi ran to Jules and held her in her arms.

"Oh, my sis," Chidi said. "We're going to get you home."

Logan shook his head. "None of you. Follow directions."

Sascha shrank into himself. "I am backup."

"Give me that gun," Logan whispered, swiping the firearm from Sascha's shaking grip. "You're nothing but a trillion-dollar liability, that's what you are."

Sascha turned to Chidi, whispering. "I talked to my therapist about the way Logan talks to me, and she thinks that internally I crave the boundaries Logan creates for me. The firm hand, if you will."

Jules perked up. "Who the fuck is... Sascha—"

"Don't say his last name," Logan said, checking security cameras. "Until he lands on American soil, no one says his damn name."

Logan cleared the exit for them as they sneaked out of the room and followed him, with Chidi and Sascha supporting Jules. She pressed her face into Chidi's shoulder as the afternoon sun blinded her.

"I've never loved the London clouds more than I do right this minute."

"We'll get you back there soon enough, sis," Chidi said, tears forming in her eyes.

~

33

The unpredictable shudders and explosions from the disturbed volcano dropped a huge boulder in front of the entrance. They were trapped inside. After being exposed to centuries of volcanic gases, lava, and heat, the surface around them was the texture of a fine onyx stone. The rock beneath their feet shook violently. Freya glanced down the huge shaft to see orange lava swirling thick chunks of volcanic rock around in bubbling circles. She didn't have to guess from the earthquakes they'd felt for days that something had reignited the long-dormant volcano. Unsettling a vengeful queen from her eternal rest might cost all of Virunga, not just Freya Blue.

Hugo pushed past Freya as a burst of gases and hot air shot in front of them from below. Hugo fell backwards before focusing on what he'd been searching for.

Freya touched one of the cracks. "We have to find a way out, or we'll be buried alive. It's going to explode." Given the amount of gases and heat coming from the inner walls, she figured they had mere minutes to get out.

She glanced up to see that the interior volcano walls were also glittering black onyx, like the stone entrance. It was Isolde's inner chamber, and she was welcoming them to their deaths. Freya stepped onto what appeared to be man-made steps, somehow carved out of the volcanic stone. She looked up and saw an effusion of gases and light battling for prominence at the very top of the opening. The volcano was now emitting a steady stream of gases. They clouded her vision. The bubbling amber lava below was rising. This was Isolde's final layer of protection.

Hugo steadied himself as he stepped slowly toward an ancient stone bridge built over the center of the volcano. The lava threatened to meet the bridge, their only path to the treasure. Freya spotted Isolde's final resting place on the other side. Glittering gold and diamonds surrounded the burial site. A yellow halo of light lit the scene through a small hole in the volcano wall, though the ominous orange tint from the bubbling lava obscured most of the light.

Hugo's eyes were fixated on the scene.

"There."

He moved toward the bridge, blinded by his desire. He stepped onto the rickety wood step that was supported by ancient woven cables. Unlike the fine surface of the stone at the entrance, the cables were barely secured to the steps. He made his way to the center of the bridge before the bridge swayed suddenly and he fell over the side. He just caught a frayed cable before falling, then dangled above the lava bubbling up from below. He cried out, then almost seemed to laugh before securing himself and climbing back onto the still swinging bridge.

A new light came into focus as Freya gazed at the scene.

Wrapped in layers of white cloth lay the remains of Isolde and her daughter. Left exposed were their hands, blackened, but intact from the volcano's gases and soils. One of her hands gripped her daughter's smaller one. In the other was the sparkling light of her diamond. Upon seeing it, Freya knew what she was tasked with doing. "Save Binta and my sisters. You can have me."

Freya stepped onto the bridge toward Hugo, determined to stop him.

34

Freya marked the moment when Hugo spotted the diamond. The massive rock lay untouched, save for the tight grasp of Isolde's hand wrapped around it. Long, blackened fingernails spun out in circles from Isolde's fingers.

"The diamond." Hugo began laughing maniacally, as he stepped off the bridge to Isolde's side. "I made it, you bastard." Freya assumed Hugo's mumbling was directed toward the spirit of his abusive father. She was halfway across the bridge when he turned and faced her.

"Thank you for getting us here," he smiled, laughing. "I don't think I'll be needing the services of the Blue sisters any longer." He grabbed the bridge cable near him and shook it until Freya lost her footing.

She grabbed the end of a frayed cable and clung to it. Freya felt the burning sensation and screamed, as the edges of her clothing singed from the heat.

"I would stay and watch, but I have better things to do."

Hugo laughed as he turned back to Isolde's resting place to claim the diamond.

The heat rose through her body, yet Freya managed to swing herself to the edge of the bridge and crawl onto its edge. Suddenly Hugo was on top of her, both of his hands wrapped tightly around her neck. Freya gasped and grabbed at his face, but she was running out of energy and oxygen. As her vision blurred, her instincts came alive. She kicked Hugo's feet from under him, causing him to fall onto the stone steps. One of the bridge cables broke loose from Isolde's side. Hugo cried out, torn between his last chance to grab what he'd come for, and ending the life of the person who brought him there. They spun with the swaying of the bridge as the lava rose to the edge of the steps.

Hugo stood and kicked Freya until she was dangling over the edge. With the weight overtaking the bridge, Freya sank lower and lower, until her feet nearly touched the lava. Bubbles rose up and scalded her ankles and she cried out. She held on with mere fingertips as Hugo got his footing and rose above her. He moved swiftly across the bridge and ripped the diamond from Isolde's grip until he clutched it in his own. Freya heard a screeching echo reverberate throughout the volcano as the diamond was taken. She felt the lava bubble up once more.

Hugo made his way back onto the swaying bridge. He stopped and placed his foot over Freya's hand as she struggled to keep hold.

"It's pathetic. What we are led to believe is a great human being—Freya Blue — now dangles over a fiery pit. Every time someone boasts or tells me of their accomplishments, I will remember this moment. And I will question it. Is that person really great? Or are they merely a poor excuse for a human being? It's the latter for you, Freya Blue." Hugo pressed his foot on top of Freya's slight grip. Freya cried out. She felt her grip loosen.

In the corner of her eye, she saw a white light rise above Isolde and her daughter. It towered over the embalmed corpses and took the form of the once-elegant Isolde. The apparition's eyes opened, revealing an amber light like that of the lava. The lava stopped rising and started to shrink lower. The scalding stopped. Then the lava rose around the sides of the volcano's shaft. The light grew clear, and Freya heard the deafening scream once more as Isolde's spirit flew from its place and enveloped Hugo in a white-orange glow.

Hugo's body, wrapped in Isolde's angry spirit, rose and shook violently. The diamond fell from his hand and Freya caught it, just as it was about to drop into the lava below. A newfound energy and strength filled Freya. Moments before she was struggling to keep a grasp on the rope keeping her alive, she now had the strength of ten and pulled herself up the side of the bridge.

Freya stood near Isolde's corpse, as her spirit wrapped around Hugo and the skin burned from his scalp and face. The diamond glowed red in Freya's hand, and she was snapped back to the present. She turned to Isolde's corpse and gently laid the diamond in the blackened remains of her hand. The glow from the diamond faded, and a light from the back of the volcano appeared, revealing an exit for Freya to escape. She raced for the exit, but stopped short of leaving, turning instead to see Isolde's spirit spin around Hugo, finishing its work until there was nothing but dust that fell into the bottom of the volcano. The lava began to rise again, overtaking the bridge that she just stepped from.

Isolde's spirit took a long glance at her, before returning to its resting place. The volcano filled with steam that rose to the opening at the top. It was clear to Freya that if the diamond had been taken, the jungle as she knew it would be forever changed by ash and lava.

Freya took one last look at the scene before squeezing through the opening and leaping off a ledge, landing on the rocky back side of the volcano. She looked up and the hole she had just slid through sealed before her eyes. The light of the afternoon beat down upon her head, and she was glad for it. Despite lack of food and water, she felt remnants of the renewed energy the diamond had imbued her with. But as soon as her feet hit the ground, she felt the sensation of falling and then rolling and then her body was dropping through a canopy of green. She grasped at tree limbs as her body continued to fall through air until she finally landed on a bed of moss at the base of a tree.

Everything ached, but she was alive. Or was she? She tried to lift her head, and the world spun around her. A light rustling brought her attention to the jungle brush. Freya braced herself for the final attack from the albino Silverback, but instead, Binta's familiar face appeared over hers. He lifted her hand to his chest and kissed it. The familiar scent of the ape reminded her of home and everything she cherished.

You made it, Freya signed. Tears filled the corners of her eyes as the thought of Chidi and Jules being threatened by Hugo's demise. *Let's go home*, Freya signed. But when she tried to get up, her vision went black, and her body began to give out. The last thing she remembered thinking was that she had kept her promise to Isolde. Had Isolde kept her sisters safe? As her mind faded into nothingness, she could only hope.

35

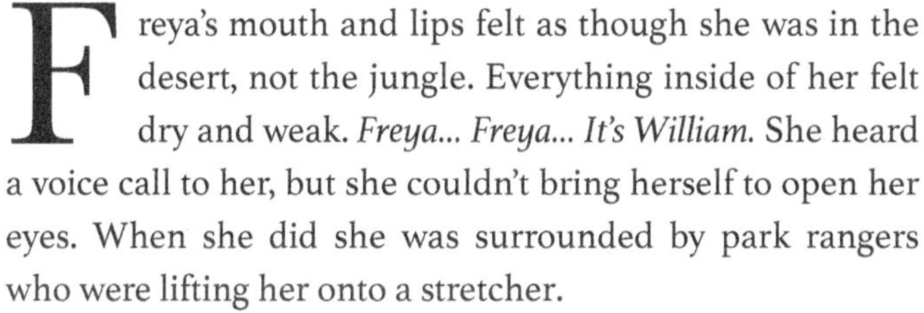

Freya's mouth and lips felt as though she was in the desert, not the jungle. Everything inside of her felt dry and weak. *Freya... Freya... It's William.* She heard a voice call to her, but she couldn't bring herself to open her eyes. When she did she was surrounded by park rangers who were lifting her onto a stretcher.

William stood over her. "You're going to be okay. Thanks to Binta here."

Freya glanced at the scene, and William came into focus. Binta sat in the background, keeping watch over their every move as they carefully carried the stretcher down the makeshift path Hugo's men had paved.

"Is he...?" She suddenly tried to sit up, panicked at the memory of Hugo.

"Rest yourself, child," William said, as the group made their way to the lowlands.

A ranger offered her hydration, and she gulped down the water.

"Mr. Lacort… we haven't located his remains as of yet. We are conducting a search."

"There were others," Freya struggled to say.

"We are aware," William said. "We're looking for them now."

"Don't… bother searching for Lacort," Freya whispered. "You won't find him."

William and the others took in what she was saying and quietly acknowledged what they all knew: Isolde had taken him for herself. The unexplained would continue to define the Congo, and its inhabitants would continue to keep her secrets close to their hearts.

"You have some family eagerly awaiting your return." William smiled.

"Jules?"

"Your room will be right next to hers in the hospital," he said.

"Maybe put me a few rooms away," Freya said. "She might go ahead and kill me herself, after what's happened."

William laughed and glanced up at Binta, who was bounding through the trees, just beside the group.

"It is nice to know that Beno and Jean didn't die in vain," William said.

Freya covered her eyes. "I tried to… I thought he might… Oh, I'm so sorry."

William glanced at the ground. "You tried to save him. It is not your fault. None of this was."

The group was silent as they made their way to the base of the volcano, where a helivac was waiting to fly Freya to the hospital. As it lifted into the air, Freya could still see the smoke rising from the volcano where Isolde was once again at peace in her final resting place.

36

Chidi looked down and sighed. She pierced an olive with a cocktail stick and set it inside the martini before carrying the tray into Jules' hospital room. Jules looked surprisingly vibrant after a good night's rest and lots of hydration. She reached out her hands and grabbed the cocktail, sighing as she took her first sip.

"The doctor said to take it slowly," Chidi said.

"Fuck that," Jules said. "I need a steady drip of vodka until I set foot on UK soil, where I belong. Then I can detox."

Her room was filled with a bustling group of millennials and older men in suits, who surrounded Sascha while Logan looked on in amusement.

Sascha scratched the back of his head. "Susie, will you look into... I want to... let's set up shop here, you know? I think it suits me. I mean, Elon went to Austin. Bezos went to D.C. I'm gonna go to... the Congo."

"You got it, boss." Susie focused on her laptop before taking a call.

"What is she..." Chidi watched in amazement. "So you can have literally anything you want. Anything that pops into your head. Just like that?"

"Pretty much, yeah," Sascha said, without a hint of sarcasm. "Although a general sense of calm has eluded me most of my life. So, there's a rather steep tradeoff."

"We've secured an office space in Kinshasa, boss," Susie said. "We've delegated some of the engineering and ops team to this branch. They're hopping on a plane shortly."

"And just like that," Jules said, sipping her martini. "You know, you might need PR services for your Kinshasa office debut. I can help with that. From London, of course."

"Susie," Sascha said. "You heard the lady."

"Well that concludes my services for you, then," Logan said, smiling. "Oh god, I feel like I can breathe again!"

"What are you talking about?" Sascha asked.

"I'm based in Palo Alto," Logan quipped, defiant.

"But you work for me."

"Ain't no way I'm coming back here," Logan said. "No offense, ladies."

"Susie, cancel it!" He turned to Chidi. "Some things I have to work for." He stepped over the group and turned to Logan. "I'll meet you at the airfield. Chidi, Jules, it's been fun. Truly. Next time you want to get kidnapped, I'm... no, I'm not here for it." He stalked off as his handlers rushed after him.

"I am going to offer him my services regardless," Jules said. "I'm not letting that account go."

Logan and Chidi laughed as Freya appeared at Jules' door with two nurses pushing her in a wheelchair.

Freya broke into tears at the sight of Jules. "Can you ever forgive me?"

37

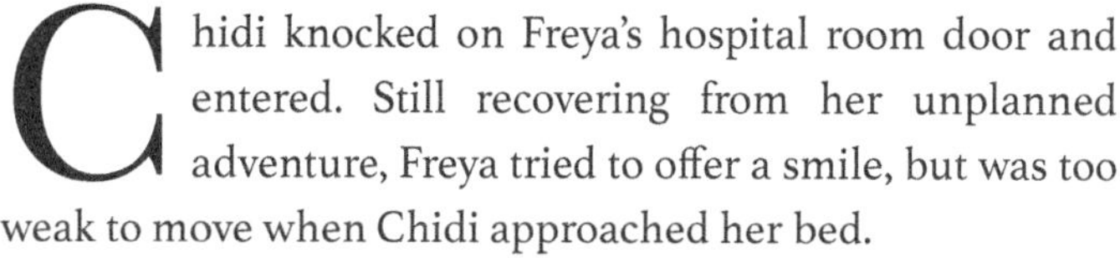

Chidi knocked on Freya's hospital room door and entered. Still recovering from her unplanned adventure, Freya tried to offer a smile, but was too weak to move when Chidi approached her bed.

"How are you feeling?" Chidi asked.

"Traumatized," Freya said. "There has been a constant stream of doctors parading in and out. I can't get a wink of sleep."

Chidi sat down, careful to avoid Freya's sore limbs. "So are you going to tell me? What happened up there?"

Freya thought back to the past few days and all that had happened. "It was all like a dream. More like a nightmare, really. And I saw things that I..." Freya stumbled to get the words out. "I saw things that make me question if what I'm seeing every day, everything I study is real at all."

"You saw her," Chidi said, smiling.

"I was also tripping off my ass from a run in with a psychotropic plant, but yes," Freya said. "I saw her."

"That is all you need to say to me," Chidi said.

Another voice chimed in from the doorway. "If I had a say about it, I would suggest that Freya's been tripping off her ass since we were kids." Jules held fast to the door for support before entering the room and sitting on the opposite side of Freya's bed. The three laughed and Freya grabbed her hand.

"You forgive me, then?" Freya asked, smiling.

Jules squeezed her hand. "It seems I do."

"But you're never booking me for a speaking engagement again, I guess," Freya said.

Jules pursed her lips, holding back a laugh. "I'm not going to bite into that one. Now, I don't know about you ladies, but I'm ready to tear it up in downtown Kinshasa."

"Right," Chidi said, laughing.

"I never thought I would be back here. Now I —"

"Never want to come back," Chidi said. "You're a city gal. We get it."

"I don't know. I suppose it would be good to get back to my jungle roots," Jules quipped. "I don't think I would've survived the city without it."

Jules climbed in beside Freya, and Chidi sat nearby on the side, holding both their hands. Tears streamed down her cheeks. "I just can't believe... yesterday I thought I'd lost you both."

Logan appeared at the door. "What a familiar scene."

He caught Freya's gaze. She held out her hand, and he sat beside her. There was an awkward tension for a minute until he stood up and scratched his head.

Freya reached out her hand to him. "Get back here. You're a Blue whether you like it or not. It's a life sentence."

"You didn't tell me that when I signed on," Logan said, taking her hand and squeezing it.

"It's a trick, really," Chidi said. "I learned early on with Howard. Once a Blue, always a Blue."

Logan held Freya's gaze and sat beside her. Chidi nodded toward the door, then helped Jules to her feet.

They closed the door behind them.

ACKNOWLEDGMENTS

Thank you to my patient and encouraging editor, Stephen Parolini, who helped me bring Freya to life. Thanks also to my fellow bookworm friends, Kadie and Whitney, for answering endless questions about potential characters and book covers.

ABOUT THE AUTHOR

C.E. Vincent is the author of the Blue Sisters Series.

Visit www.cevincentauthor.com or scan the QR code below to sign up for her newsletter and hear about C.E.'s latest releases and signing events.

Find C.E. Vincent on:

www.ingramcontent.com/pod-product-compliance
Lightning Source LLC
LaVergne TN
LVHW050640100826
845148LV00011B/1917